The
Magician's
Apprentice

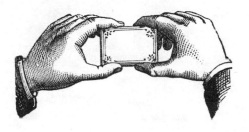

The
Magician's
Apprentice

JUDITH
HENEGHAN

HOLIDAY HOUSE / New York

© 2005 by Judith Heneghan
First published in the United Kingdom in 2005
as *Stonecipher* by Andersen Press Limited,
20 Vauxhall Bridge Road, London SWIV 2SA
First published in the United States of America
by Holiday House, Inc. in 2008
All Rights Reserved
Printed in the United States of America
www.holidayhouse.com
1 3 5 7 9 10 8 6 4 2

Library of Congress Cataloging-in-Publication Data

Heneghan, Judith.
The magician's apprentice / by Judith Heneghan.
p. cm.
Summary: In 1874 Winchester, England, Jago Stonecipher, magician's assistant to his
unscrupulous uncle, becomes involved in a series of plots and deceits revolving around a
lady's maid and her employer's family, and finally escapes to sea, where the trouble follows
him, even aboard ship.
ISBN 978-0-8234-2150-3 (hardcover)
[1. Swindlers and swindling—Fiction.   2. Adventure and adventurers—Fiction.
3. Magicians—Fiction.   4. Orphans—Fiction.   5. Winchester (England)—
History—19th century—Fiction.   6. Great Britain—History—Victoria,
1837–1901—Fiction.]   I. Title.
PZ7.H3866Mag 2008
[Fic]—dc22
2007035186

For Paul

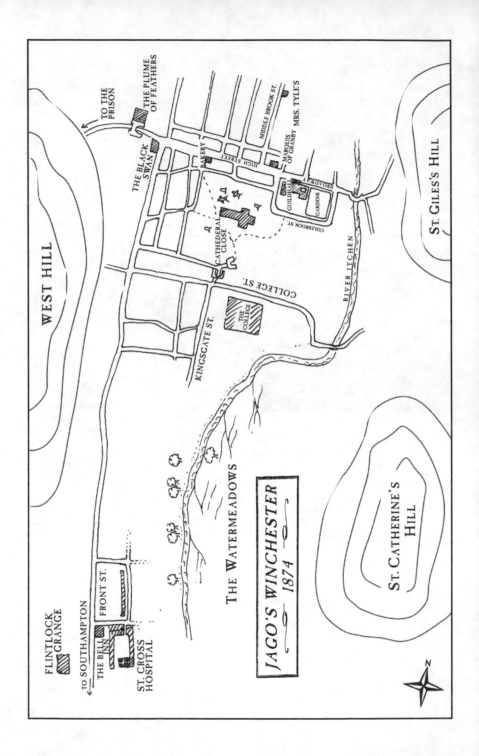

Contents

Part One

Flesh and
Blood

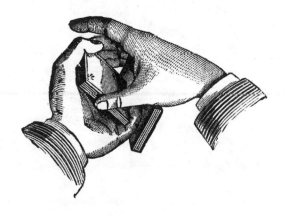

1
August 1874

Jago waited in the ragged shade of a hawthorn tree. The sun's white glare made him squint. He shut his eyes, leaned back against the twisted trunk and let the hawkers' shouts wash over him.

"Pups for sale! Not a mongrel among 'em!"

"All the way from London, ladies! Tortoiseshell buttons!"

The fair had been busy since dawn. High up on the chalky downland above Winchester, the grass was already well trampled and the air was thick with the pungent stink of sweat and country cheese. Stallholders mopped their brows and swigged warm beer from big pint pots. Children ran about with sticky handfuls of lardy cake, shrieking at the wasps.

Jago's stomach rumbled painfully. He hadn't eaten since the day before. As usual, he'd have to earn his dinner. Not yet though—he knew he had to wait for the signal.

"Right then! You, sir! You, madam! What's the 'urry? You'll be awful sorry if you pass me by! Stop right here for the experience of a lifetime!"

A hoarse voice crackled above the drifting crowds. Jago opened one eye. Across the hillside the old man was setting up shop. He wasn't yet sixty, but he was worn out, frayed and stooping with rheumatism. Jago watched as he dusted down his stained frock coat, stepped painfully onto his crate and clapped his hands above the bobbing hats and bonnets.

"No doubt you've all heard of me, but just in case there are any dimwits among you, I am Archibald Callow, Master of Miraculous Marvels and Diviner of Supernatural Phenomena!"

A handful of passersby dawdled just long enough to catch the old man's eye. He coughed and spat out a large gob of phlegm by way of clearing his throat.

"Now you ladies and you gentlemen aren't stupid, are you? No, you're all far too clever for any cheapskate trickery-pokery . . ."

The heat seemed to be pressing itself into the hillside. Jago shifted uncomfortably as Callow wiped his sweating face with his sleeve.

" . . . So what I've prepared for you today is a spectacle so daring, so hor-dacious that you will gasp, tremble and, ladies, perhaps even faint!"

"Oh get on with it, you old codger!" The heckler was a young girl selling fruit from a nearby barrow.

"Brat!" growled Callow as he opened up a large black doctor's bag on the rickety table in front of him. "Now then. There are a few grisly secrets in 'ere, I can tell you. Take this for instance."

He rummaged around in the bag, pulled out a rusting old sword and held it up for his audience to admire. "This blade, my friends, was waggled at old Boneyparts by the Duke of Marlborough 'imself!"

"Friend of yours, is he?" jeered the girl. The crowd tittered, and a few more onlookers moved away, more intent on finding shade than watching a second-rate traveling showman's tricks.

"Go on, walk away!" shouted Callow, waving the sword at their backs. "No guts! It takes a braver soul than you to witness the Miracle of One Thousand Cuts!" With a loud grunt he heaved the bag in front of him onto its side. Knives, swords, blades of every description clattered out onto the table. "Oh yes! And it takes a truly extra-hordinary type to undertake the ordeal 'imself! Now then, what I need is a volunteer. . . ."

Callow's dry shouting rose above the heads of the browsers and hawkers and dissolved in the heat. Farther down the hillside, among the butchers' wagons and haberdashery stalls, no one could hear him. Jago knew better, however. He stood up and began to stroll in the old man's direction. The barrowmen eyed him suspiciously as he passed their vegetable stacks and crates of scrabbling hens. Grubby and ragged, he obviously had no money. All street boys were nothing but dirty little thieves.

Callow, meanwhile, was busy handing out the knives and blades from his bag to doubtful onlookers.

"Test them yourselves!" he was insisting. "Only I won't be liable for any injuries. . . . These blades are one 'undred percent genuine, and yet the volunteer will walk away, miraculously unharmed. For this astonishing feat I require an assistant of exceptional courage and hor-dacity! If you think you're brave enough, step forward now!"

The crowd fell silent. For a moment it looked as though no one would volunteer. Then, in a clear, confident voice, Jago spoke up.

"I'll do it."

The crowd, growing now, made way for him as he walked up to Callow's makeshift stage.

"And what is your name, my boy?" asked Callow as he turned him round to face his audience.

"Jago Stonecipher, sir."

"Well, Stonecipher, you're a bold lad. How old are you? Twelve? Thirteen? Believe you me, what you are about to live through is not for the faint 'earted! Now, I want you to step inside this cabinet for a moment. I will shut the door. You must stand absolutely still. One movement and, well . . ." He rolled his eyes. "We don't want you to lose your head, do we?"

The cabinet in question was nothing more than a large, upended traveling trunk. It had been painted black. Across the top a handwritten sign declared HE WHO ENTERS DICES WITH DEATH in scrawling red script. Callow opened the door and Jago stepped inside without hesitating. The old conjuror closed the door quickly and secured it with a large padlock.

"Are you comfortable in there?" called Callow, banging on the door.

"Comfortable enough!" came the reply from inside.

"Then I shall begin!"

Callow selected a long carving knife from the pile on the table and tested the blade with his thumb. "Razor sharp!"

He then stepped up to the side of the cabinet and paused, feeling the thin board with his fingers. By now the audience had swelled to a sizable crowd. Curiosity had got the better of many, and the boy's cool nerve heightened the drama, so there was a collective intake of breath when Callow lined up the first knife and thrust it sharply through the cabinet wall.

Inside the trunk, Jago's eyes were still adjusting to the dark. When Callow shut the door, his practiced fingers had swiftly found the hidden catch to the secret compartment at the back. He squeezed himself into its cramped space by squatting down with his head bent between his knees. It wasn't difficult. He was so thin there wasn't much of him to hide. It was stiflingly hot though; there was little air and he sucked in his breath in short gasps. Yet Jago hadn't expected anything else. Callow was his uncle. The two of them had worked this trick a hundred times before.

He could hear the knives being inserted through wood above his shoulders. They struck against each other, metal ringing on metal. The sound echoed in his head with a dull throb.

Outside, Callow was treating the crowd to a description of the French guillotine—the way the blade sliced, the victim's head rolled and the blood spilled. Jago's stomach churned. He bit his lips. He wasn't sure if it was hunger or heat or his uncle's crude performance that made him feel sick. There was no art to the old man's tricks; he had little skill as an illusionist. The show was a sham, and the crowd watched merely to see if he drew blood. Sometimes they got what they wanted if the knives went in too quick. Callow might be Jago's only surviving relative, but Jago had a whole cartload of reasons for hating him.

The heat inside the trunk was becoming unbearable. Jago's head pounded and he shut his eyes. If he screwed them up tightly enough, he could see his sister Clara in his mind's eye. She was sitting by the window with a book in her hands. Something by Mr. Dickens, no doubt. She began to read, the story falling like a lullaby from her lips.

"Whether I shall turn out to be the hero of my own life, or whether that station will be held by anybody else, these pages must show . . ."

This was how Jago protected himself. Eyes shut, he wove a magic cloak of words, mouthing the phrases he remembered so clearly, wrapping himself in the soothing balm of his sister's phantom voice.

When the last sword had been inserted, Callow tapped on the side of the trunk.

"Are you alive, young Stonecipher?" Jago didn't answer. He wasn't supposed to. Callow reckoned it heightened the tension.

"Is he dead?" asked a woman in the crowd.

"Unlikely so soon." Callow leered. "Knife wounds bleed long and slow y'see. . . . Is there a physician in the audience?"

Jago heard the blades above him being withdrawn. His head was spinning. He knew he was supposed to crawl back into the main part of the trunk, but he found he couldn't move his arms. From somewhere in the distance, he heard Callow fumble with the padlock and open the outer door. Now there'd be trouble. . . .

"He's done a runner! Scampered out the back!"

"You should be paying us to watch this rubbish!"

The crowd laughed as the barrow girl started hurling rotten apples.

"Bleedin' little strapper!" hissed the old man through a crack in the trunk. "I'll knock your block off for this!"

Yet Jago barely heard him. His ears were filling with a roaring, rushing sound like an autumn gale through an empty wood that howled about his head until he could bear no more. Only then did he black out, fainting into the comfort of silence and nothingness.

2
Beside the Graveyard

"Watch the cart! If anyone touches it, I'll 'ave yer guts for garters!" Callow gave Jago a quick clip around the ear. "And no more of yer swooning and fainting!"

It was late evening. The molten sun had finally sunk behind the cathedral. Callow had the promise of a bed at Mrs. Tyle's threepenny lodgings but he had told Jago that he fancied a drink first and was off to the Plume of Feathers for some liquid refreshment. The old man had made it pretty clear that he didn't want the drunks spilling out from the pubs at closing time to get their thieving hands on any of his property, so he had left his cart in a quiet spot near the cathedral, just beyond the graveyard perimeter, with Jago to guard it.

As the night darkened, the air grew cooler. Jago climbed in among the battered trunks and bric-a-brac and pulled an old piece of tarpaulin over him. His shoulders ached. Callow had once had a pony to pull the cart, but since the animal's death a few weeks ago Jago had had to haul the props around himself. The old man treated him like a slave. He thought he could rough him up when he felt like it and Jago would be too scared to fight back. Jago, though, knew different. He was skinny all right, but he wasn't weak. He knew that one day, when he'd learned enough, when he was strong enough he would run away and it wouldn't be to the workhouse or the bottom of the heap in some thieving street gang either. He had a plan. He would wait and leave Callow only when he was ready.

Jago shivered under the tarpaulin. When Callow was drunk he often jeered about their relationship: "We're family, my boy! You're not goin' to creep off now, are you? Blood's thicker than water!" Such talk hurt more than the beatings, in a way. Callow might be his uncle, but that didn't make him special. Clara had been special.

Jago took something out of his pocket. It was a block of printer's type. *J* for Jago—a thumb-sized wedge of wood with the metal letter raised on one side. He traced its smooth cold curves with his finger. His sister, Clara, had once swept the floors in a printing works. She had given him the letter-block, and now it was all he had left of her. Times Roman, she'd called it. It was his talisman.

He turned it over in his hand and practiced a few sleight-of-hand tricks in the darkness. Make it disappear. Reappear. Disappear again. The dark helped him to hone his skills. He had to *feel* the letter-block between his thumb and forefinger, into the palm, a quick flick up his sleeve and then back again. The movements became faster and faster, rhythmic, almost invisible. And it felt good.

In Market Street, just beyond the almshouses that bordered the northern side of the cathedral, the lamplighter was making his rounds. Horses' hooves clattered on the cobbles as people made their way home to bed. Few folk used the shortcut past the graveyard after dark, however. There were no gas lamps here and the looming mass of the cathedral blotted out the stars. Soon everything was quiet. Jago was tired and fell into a deep sleep.

Clara was lying by the dying embers in the grate. Her hair was damp with sweat and her skin glistened palely. Jago held a book in his hands, trying to read to her but the words on the page kept jumping about in front of him. She tossed her head feverishly and groaned. Jago was making her ill. He couldn't read and it was his fault that she was ill. If only he could get the words to make sense then everything would be all right.

"Don't die!" he pleaded silently. "Don't leave me on my own!"

Clara was shivering but there was no more coal, no more warmth, no more words.

Jago woke up and his dreams fled. He could see nothing in the inky blackness. There was a dank, moldy smell and his neck felt stiff.

However, the voice that had woken him was real enough.

"Please! Try to understand!" A girl was speaking, hushed and whispering, but urgent. A man's voice, deeper, impatient, cut her off.

"What is there to understand?"

Jago stayed still under the tarpaulin. He guessed that the speakers were probably standing right next to the cart and he didn't want to be found. There was probably some law about not spending the night on the cathedral grounds. Callow would be furious if he came back and found that his props had been impounded by an overeager police constable. The couple, however, didn't seem too concerned about the tatty old cart beside them.

"He left me *nothing.*" The man sounded bitter. "He gambled his entire fortune on that one bogus investment and lost it all. There isn't a penny left for me."

"Do you think they might catch the thieves who swindled him?"

The man laughed hollowly.

"Armbruster doesn't reckon the rule of law means much in Brazil."

There was a pause and then the girl spoke again, hesitantly, cautious now.

"I . . . I don't trust Armbruster. Miss Piggott won't even speak to him. But I can't talk about him here. I came to give you this. Your father would want you to have it, I think."

Jago was getting pins and needles. He needed to move. He stretched out one leg and pushed his shoulders back, causing the tarpaulin to shift a fraction. A gap appeared and Jago could just make out the huddled mass of two figures standing an arm's length away. The taller figure, shoulders hunched, was holding something in his hand.

"My father's watch! Where did you find this?"

"I think Miss Piggott must have forgotten about it." The girl's voice dropped to a whisper. She drew close to the man, muffling her words into the darkness of his silhouette. "There's something else . . . the key—I took it. Don't say anything. . . . I know he meant it for you."

"I'm taking the first boat out of Southampton!" The man pulled away suddenly, banging his clenched fist against the railing.

"Don't be too hasty, please! Don't make me regret taking them!" The girl fell silent. From somewhere farther off came the sound of footsteps crunching on gravel. She turned her head, but it was too dark for Jago to see either of their faces. "Someone is coming. I must go."

"Anna . . ."

"Later. Good-bye!"

And then the girl was gone. Yet no one else came along the path. The footsteps had stopped, or gone in a different direction.

Jago needed to get out of the cart to stretch his legs, but the man was still standing by the railing. The two were obviously caught up in some messy affair over money. Jago couldn't imagine what it might feel like to inherit anything, unless it was a lifetime of toil and black eyes. The rich always wanted to be richer. Why didn't the man just go home?

The figure by the railing was looking at something he held in his hand. Then, without warning, he raised his arm and hurled the object over the railing into the graveyard beyond. There was a glint of metal as the moon briefly glanced it, followed by a faint clink. It must have hit a gravestone somewhere out in the darkness.

The man, however, hadn't stayed to hear it fall. All that was left was the echo of his footsteps fading swiftly into the night.

"Get up, yer lazy sod!"

Callow yanked off the tarpaulin and the bright morning sunlight stabbed at Jago's eyes. Before he could move,

Callow grabbed his arm and was pulling him out of the cart, shouting and ranting.

"You were supposed to be watching the props, not dozing and snoring like a pig in clover!"

Callow stank of gin. His eyes were bloodshot and he staggered about, swiping at Jago and cursing. He had obviously been boozing all night. Jago stepped swiftly out of his range.

"Go and get me something to eat. Me back's killing me and now I'll have to make sure nobody nabbed anything while you were having your pretty little beauty sleep!"

Food would help the old man to sober up, but Jago didn't have any money so he ran off toward the High Street to pinch a bit of breakfast. A couple of pies would do the trick. Clara wouldn't have liked it though. She hadn't stolen anything in all her short life, which was why Jago was careful never to take more than he needed to keep body and soul together. This made him a lousy thief in Callow's eyes, but Jago often wondered how it would feel to walk into a shop and pay good money, coins on the counter and no shenanigans, for an honest loaf of bread.

All the same, stealing food had cost him dearly along the way, what with the beatings and the thrashings, not to mention the greengrocer who locked him in his coal cellar for two whole days. So Jago had developed a strategy. He never stole anything without asking for it first. This refinement, along with his ability to distract any witnesses (developed over the years by watching Callow's more inventive rivals on the traveling showman's circuit), served him well.

On this particular morning Jago strolled into the bakery by the old Buttercross with his eye on a couple of large onion pies. The shop was crowded. The baker's wife looked overheated as she counted out a dozen currant buns from a tray in the window. Jago could have taken the pies without anyone noticing at all. His instinct, however, was to perform.

"Excuse me, 'scuse me!" he called, pushing his way to the front of the line. An old woman standing next to the counter was busy stowing a small cottage loaf in her basket.

"Wait your turn!" she scolded as Jago reached forward and picked up a glass saltcellar that sat on the countertop for the benefit of the customers. He turned to face the muttering crowd behind him.

"Been waiting long?" he asked.

"Get out of the way! Push off!" shouted a man in a coachman's livery from the back of the line, but the people nearest the counter were too busy watching Jago's right hand to complain. For when he raised his arm and opened his fingers to let go of the saltcellar, it didn't fall to the floor as it should have done. Instead it appeared to be floating immediately beneath Jago's middle finger. He moved his hand through the air in a smooth, sweeping arc and the saltcellar followed, hovering with it as though under the influence of some invisible force.

"It's levitating!" breathed a young errand boy, happily diverted from his long list of morning messages.

Jago directed the saltcellar back down to the counter and then raised his hand to show that there was no secret piece of string. The thin piece of wire he had lowered from his sleeve, concealed beneath his middle finger and jammed into the top of the saltcellar was already safely back under his jacket. There was no mystery or even cleverness in the mechanics of the trick; its success depended entirely on the practiced art of the performer. Callow generally avoided such close-up magic. His crippled fingers weren't supple enough, and he found it easier to employ the shock tactics of knives and gory tales. "Go for the jugular!" he'd say, but Jago preferred a lighter touch.

"Do it again!" pleaded the errand boy, and several other customers murmured their agreement.

"Do what again?" The baker's wife had finished tying string around the box of buns and was staring at Jago across the counter. "What are you doing with my salt-cellar?"

"I've been entertaining your customers," answered Jago. "And I was just wondering if you might give me something for my trouble?"

"What?" The baker's wife didn't look too pleased. "Get out of here, you scruffy little tyke!"

Same as usual. He'd asked politely and all he'd got was rudeness. He told himself that she deserved what happened next. A woman standing behind Jago screamed suddenly.

"Aaargh! Get off! Get off!" She started to hop about, waving her arms and tugging at her heavy skirts. "There's a rat in here! I felt it run over my foot!"

The baker's wife leaned over the counter, ready to stamp on the offending creature.

"Where did it go?"

While the baker was summoned to deal with the rat

17

and his wife appeased her indignant customers, Jago slipped out of the shop with two warm pies in his pockets. There was no rat. He had merely brushed his toe across the top of the woman's shoe. It wasn't exactly difficult; all it took was an ability to play on the fear of the customers in the shop. Jago had got his breakfast but he felt vaguely ashamed. Deceit was Callow's game. A real illusionist worked with his audience, not against them.

As Jago ran down Colebrook Street and turned back up toward the cathedral he remembered the couple he'd overheard by the railing the night before. He slowed down and took a bite out of one of the pies. As the warm food took the edge off his hunger he grew more curious. What had the man thrown away? He had been given a watch and a key. A key was worth nothing, but a watch— well, even a broken watch might have some value. Jago checked to see that no one was watching before he climbed over the railing.

The pockmarked gravestones skewed in all directions like blackened, rotting teeth. Bodies weren't buried here anymore. These days the dead ended up in neat rows in new graveyards at a more sanitary distance from the city center. The remaining memorials were covered with moss and lichen, gray and ancient like the immovable mass of the cathedral behind them. Yet the ground was still sacred. Jago didn't dawdle. The cathedral wardens regularly patrolled the perimeter and they weren't exactly a friendly bunch.

Jago soon found what he was looking for. At the base of a thickly crusted headstone lay a gentleman's gold fob watch on a linked gold chain. The glass had smashed and the watch had stopped. The back had broken open on impact and one of its small brass cogs lay beside it in the grass. Jago picked up the pieces. The gold would still be worth a fair bit.

Then he noticed the letter. A sheet of paper had been folded into a small square and hidden in the back of the watch. Jago pulled it out and opened it up. Someone had written a note in capital letters.

I KNOW WHAT ARMBRUSTER DID. MEET
ME AT SAINT CROSS AFTER EVENSONG
TOMORROW. ANNA.

Clara had taught Jago his letters before she died of cholera in their little room near the docks at Portsmouth. He had a good memory. He saw the shapes of words though he'd never told Callow that he could read. He knew perfectly well that the old man would simply view his learning as a quick route to some new racket. For Jago, his ability to read was like a trick up his sleeve. He kept it hidden, and maybe one day he'd find a use for it.

Right now, however, he didn't have time to dawdle over hidden messages. A black-cassocked warden was striding toward him, shouting and gesticulating, so Jago thrust the note in his pocket, leaped back over the railing and ran off toward Callow and the cart.

Callow was peeing noisily against a wall.

"What've you got for me then?" He snatched his pie with his free hand. "And what else've you got there?"

Callow had seen the watch. Jago swiftly concealed it up

19

his sleeve but he was too late. The old man grabbed his elbow with a surprisingly strong grip.

"Trying to teach an old dog new tricks, eh? Hand it over."

Jago saw no point in arguing and did as he was told.

"So, you've finally come round to the notion of some proper picky-pocketing, 'ave you?" Callow chuckled as he examined the watch. "About time too! You've got to do better than this though. Broken tickers don't fetch nearly as much."

"I didn't nick it. I found it."

"Eh? Oh well, call it what you like. Presh—prestidigitation—that's the dandys' word for it. But this'll make a pretty little trick for today's show. We'll see what it's worth later, shall we? Maybe there'll be a coin or two in it for you. You'd better get the cart over to Mrs. Tyle's place before she gives my bed to someone else." And with that, Callow pocketed the watch and staggered off in search of a pitch for the day.

3
Armbruster

Jago knew where he'd find Callow. He threaded his way down the busy High Street to the bottom end of town. There, in front of the new guildhall, the old man was already trying to catch himself a crowd. It was a good pitch, but a risky one. The broad street was lined with the carriages and carts of people doing business in the city, while strollers ambled through the gates of the neighboring public gardens with time on their hands and coins in their pockets. The problem was the guildhall. Its mock-gothic arches and turreted roof housed the city council chambers, and everyone knew that some councillors were less keen on roadside amusements than others.

"Come on, ladies and gents! What about a bit of juggle-mongering? 'Ave you ever seen five shillings transmutated into ten? Pick a card, any card! You, sir, what about finding an egg under your 'at? No? You don't fancy being able to surprise the missus with it later? I've made the Prince of Wales 'imself smile with that one!"

After the fiasco with the Miracle of One Thousand Cuts the day before, Callow had decided to stick with smaller tricks for a while. Fewer props also meant a quicker escape, if necessary.

"No, you lot like something a bit more sophisticated, don't you! Well as it 'appens I've got just the thing for you today. If I may have a bit of 'ush now, kiddies, I shall treat you all to The Miracle of the Consumed Gold!" Callow pulled the broken watch out of his pocket and dangled it from its chain. It glinted sharply in the sunlight. "Solid gold, this is! Solid gold. . . ."

Whenever Jago wasn't needed to act as a volunteer, his job was to pass among the audience with a cap to collect any coins that might be forthcoming. Most of the time people moved out of his way, muttering about con men and swindlers and avoiding his eye. Callow would have preferred him just to pinch a few wallets, but Jago didn't think his master's performance deserved such generosity as a rule. If, however, anyone seemed to be enjoying themselves yet still refused to cough up a copper or two, he reckoned that some payment was due. This might be no more than an apple from a shopping basket. Payment in kind. And it provided him with excellent practice.

Callow was busy swallowing the gold watch. Or rather, he was leaning his head back, opening his mouth very wide and raising the arm that held the chain so that he could slip it down his coat sleeve. The crowd seemed to like this trick and Callow played them along, pretending to gag and choke as the last of the chain disappeared. Few noticed that the guildhall doors had opened and several well-dressed gentlemen had come out onto the steps above Callow's head.

Most of the group made their way toward the pump down the road where horses and carriages stood waiting. They didn't throw a second glance at the holiday crowd, and if they had, there were plenty of ladies' parasols to obscure the view. Yet one man remained at the top of the steps. He was thickset, weighty—doing well for himself too by the look of his elegant topcoat and self-satisfied smile. Perhaps he was waiting for someone. He leaned over the balcony and watched Callow's performance without interest. It must have been hot under his tall silk hat and stiff collar, for shiny beads of sweat had gathered across his broad brow.

The audience were beginning to tire of Callow's gagging antics. So, with a loud gargling sound he began to perform the trick in reverse, holding his sleeve close to his mouth and pulling out the watch on the chain with exaggerated slowness.

"And so, the watch that was consumed is . . . regurgitated!" Callow bowed, and swung the watch up for the audience to marvel at.

Then suddenly, the man on the balcony leaned forward. He was peering at something below him in the crowd. Jago watched him warily and wondered if there was going to be any trouble. Some of the more well-to-do townsfolk had taken rather a high tone lately with the itinerant showmen who came and went through the city. It was rumored that a recent council resolution had classed all unlicensed performers as criminals who should be taken out to the turnpike road or locked up for a day or two. He would have to warn Callow.

Someone tugged at Jago's shirtsleeve. He jumped, but it was only a little girl.

"My papa says here's a farthing." She put the coin very carefully into his cap. The show was over and the crowd was moving on. Jago looked up at the balcony, but the man had disappeared. It seemed that there was nothing to worry about, after all.

Callow's energy was spent and he wanted a drink. All that choking and spluttering had given him a dry throat.

"The pump's just over there," suggested Jago, stepping sideways to avoid a clip round the ear.

"Don't be stupid, boy. I mean a proper drink."

So Callow took the coins from Jago's cap and they made their way back up the High Street to the Marquis of Granby.

The Marquis of Granby was a crooked little tavern in every respect. The walls leaned out into the road and the low doorway slanted to one side. Sandwiched between two newer brick buildings, its blackened wooden beams looked like they soon might give out under the strain.

Jago had to duck his head as he followed Callow inside. The old man hobbled over to a dark corner and sat down on a wooden bench.

"What are you coming in for?" Callow didn't want Jago hanging around. "Stay outside and look after the cart."

"I left the cart at Mrs. Tyle's like you told me to."

"Well, stay outside anyway."

This instruction suited Jago just fine. He went back to the pump and had a good long drink, washed his face and wetted his head. Then he wandered between the horses watering at the trough and stroked the mane of a soulful-looking gray mare. It was only as he walked back up the High Street that he saw the top-hatted man again. He was entering the Granby, stooping low and twisting his heavy shoulders to fit through the narrow door. Jago followed, but hesitated at the threshold. He didn't want to get involved if Callow was about to be hauled off to see the magistrate.

Inside the tavern, the barman was busy clearing glasses. The room was dark and gloomy, so when a large figure loomed over the bar he was naturally startled.

"Mr. Armbruster, sir! Sorry, sir! I didn't see you come in. What can I get you, sir?"

Armbruster . . . Jago leaned back into the shadow of the doorway. Wasn't Armbruster the name in the note Jago had found? The man looked just like any other prospering gentleman of the city except for a lumpish, mottled scar beneath his left eye. It gave him the look of a prizefighter, strangely at odds with his close-fitting waistcoat and extravagant cravat.

"Nothing for now." Armbruster was replying to the barman. "I have other business to attend to."

"Of course, of course. Just let me know if you want anything, sir."

The barman scuttled out into the backyard. Jago could see that there was no one besides Armbruster and Callow in the room. Armbruster didn't waste any time. He walked over to Callow's little corner and sat down opposite him.

"I'd like to see the watch, if you don't mind."

"Eh? Who are you?" Callow peered across the table. He had already drunk several gins, judging by the empty glasses in front of him.

"Never mind who I am. I want the watch."

"I 'aven't got a watch."

"Give me the watch," repeated Armbruster, with cold emphasis.

"I tell you what," said Callow, "if you was to get me a nice little 'alf-pint measure of brandy we might be able to talk about it."

Armbruster leaned forward, kneading his fists until the bones cracked.

"I saw you prancing about with the watch this morning. Where did you get it?"

"I regurgitated it, didn't I?" Callow laughed, but the laughter stuck in his throat as Armbruster stretched across the table and grabbed Callow by the collar.

"Look, you miserable old fool, I saw you with the watch, and I saw your tricky young apprentice picking a few pockets while you played the village idiot. Now either you give me the watch or I turn you both over to the magistrate!"

Jago turned to run. He didn't want to find himself up in front of the city magistrate. Armbruster, however, seemed to have known he was there all along.

"No you don't!" He leaped up and in an instant he had covered the distance to the door, grabbed Jago's arm and dragged him into the dingy room.

"Sit there!" he snarled, pushing Jago into the seat beside Callow. "You're off to the reformatory if your addle-brained governor doesn't hand over the watch!"

Jago's arm was hurting. He looked at Callow, but the old man wasn't about to help him out.

"'Ave you been pinching stuff, boy? Shame on you!" Callow gave the side of Jago's head a slap and turned back to Armbruster. "I've told him an 'undred times, but he don't listen to a rheumy old bloke like me. A right little monkey . . ."

Jago felt the old familiar compression in his chest. He knew perfectly well that Callow didn't really care if he lived or died, but strangely, the constant betrayals didn't hurt any less. Jago had his uses for his uncle, but Callow would always save his own skin first.

Armbruster, however, wasn't fooled by Callow's side-stepping. He banged his fists onto the table, so that the empty glasses jumped.

"I've wasted enough time. I'll smash both your heads together if you don't stop mucking about!"

That was quite enough for Callow.

"All right! Keep your hair on! Maybe we did find something but we never nicked it. . . ." Jago stared sullenly at the table as Callow fumbled inside his coat and produced the battered timepiece. Armbruster snatched it up and examined it.

"Where is the note?"

This time Callow looked genuinely baffled.

"What note?"

Armbruster raised his arm, more than ready to aim a blow at Callow's head. Jago saw no point in getting pulverized, but he didn't want to let a cocky bully like Armbruster have everything his own way, either.

"I found the watch!" he shouted, though he might have held his tongue if he'd had more time to think. "I found it in the graveyard. There may have been a bit of paper, I don't know. I can't read, can I?"

At that moment the barman came back inside, doubled up under the weight of the barrel of beer across his shoulders. He set it down on the dirt floor and looked across at them. Armbruster pulled back his fist, but the poor man had seen it.

"Is everything all right, sir?" he asked, trying to keep the nerves out of his voice.

A man in a fine suit has a reputation to maintain. Armbruster was clearly not going to get any further with their "discussion" so he stood up from the table. But before he left he turned round and snarled at Callow and Jago like a dog at the end of its chain.

"If you're lying, I'll find you and I'll kill you."

4

The Trap

It was late afternoon. At Mrs. Tyle's lodging house the windows were boarded up. Callow lay downstairs on a flea-ridden mattress, hiding from the sun. He was drunk. His snores shuddered through the dingy rooms. There would be no more performances from the Master of Miraculous Marvels for a few hours, at least.

The warm air carried the stench of cracked drains out into the yard. A tatty little card pinned to the doorpost read MRS. TYLE, PROFESSIONAL MEDIUM, SÉANCES BY APPOINTMENT IN STRICTEST CONFIDENCE. On the back step sat the woman herself, smoking a pipe to ward off the stink. She wore a greasy apron and a deep country-woman's bonnet that shaded her wrinkled face. When Jago came out and shut the door quietly behind him, she barely moved.

"Sneaking off, are we?"

Jago didn't stop to chat.

"If the old man wakes up, tell him I'm treating myself to a first-rate supper at the Duke's Head," he muttered bitterly, skidding across the filthy cobbles and escaping into Middle Brook Street.

As Jago walked through the tatty little alleys to the east of the cathedral a bell tolled. Five o'clock. He dug his hands deep into the pockets of his worn-out trousers. No money, nothing to do, nowhere to go. But there was something in his pocket. A piece of paper. He pulled out the note from the watch and looked at it again.

I KNOW WHAT ARMBRUSTER DID. MEET ME AT SAINT CROSS AFTER EVENSONG TOMORROW. ANNA.

This Anna obviously knew something about Armbruster. Jago touched the bruises on his arm as he remembered how the man had threatened him earlier. What was his problem? He was nothing but a thug in fancy clothes. Callow wasn't going to wake up for a few hours, so Jago decided to take a little stroll out of town.

In Kingsgate Street he met a clutch of schoolboys. They were on their way to the cricket grounds by the look of the bat one of them was using to swipe at some sparrows.

"Excuse me, but what time is evensong at St. Cross?" Since Clara's death Jago hadn't exactly been a regular churchgoer.

"Ha! Did you hear that!" The boys clearly found Jago's question amusing. "What does a filthy mongrel like you want with evensong? After the pennies in the poor box, are you?" The speaker nudged at his friends. "Or maybe he's got a fancy to see the ladies kneeling!"

One boy, a tall lad with lank hair, gave Jago a push with his shoulder.

"Where are your manners? You ought to address us as 'sirs,' don't you think?"

"It was a civil enough question," muttered Jago, keeping his head down and skirting round the group. He walked away quickly without looking back. The tall boy laughed. He hadn't yet discovered that the shiny leather cricket ball in his kit bag had disappeared. Jago had taken it. It never paid to be rude.

At the little post office, Jago learned that evensong would be at six o'clock. He had nearly an hour to kill. He'd had enough of schoolboys and so decided to take the river path rather than the road. Perhaps he would have time to cool his feet a little in the water.

St. Cross was a small parish a mile or two south of the city. The river carved up the empty stretch of meadow that lay in between. Cows grazed on the boggy pasture. The nettles grew to waist height and the reeds that lined the narrow path rustled high above Jago's head. Anyone could walk from the city walls to St. Cross without being seen. Or they could hide or lie in wait.

Yet on a hot afternoon with the shadows from the trees lengthening across the drifting water, it seemed too peaceful to be out looking for trouble. Jago was tired. He pushed aside the brittle reeds and sat on a willow stump by the river's edge. A startled moorhen skittered across to the opposite bank. He kicked off his boots and gasped as his feet entered the cold water. Then he closed his eyes and let the weeds caress his ankles.

Why on earth was he going to St. Cross? He had read a note he shouldn't have read. It had nothing to do with him. He had enough trouble just working out where the next meal was coming from. If Armbruster had threatened him, so what? He'd been bullied and threatened most of his life. Best to stay away and not get involved. . . .

But then he heard a noise. He sat up sharply and listened to the thud of several pairs of boots approaching along the sun-baked path. With the footsteps came a harsh, cracking sound, as though someone was beating the reeds with a stick.

"Now you know what to do," said a man's voice. It was a deep voice, and familiar.

"Piggott's a weak sort of a fellow, and there are two of you. Make it quick, mind, and do it properly."

There was no mistaking that tone. Armbruster was coming. Jago reached for his boots but stayed low, crouching. The thrashing sound was getting closer. He didn't want to be discovered all alone on an otherwise deserted riverbank.

The reeds crashed under the stick. The men were almost level by now; their feet clumped steadily. Jago could hear their labored breath as he held his own. Then, suddenly, they were past him. The footsteps faded and there was no more talk. Yet he did not stand up for some time. The beating sound had receded but not his thumping heart. Armbruster was spoiling for a fight. It seemed as though someone called Piggott was in for a rough ride, and Jago knew he would go to St. Cross for evensong after all.

He waited until he felt confident that he wouldn't be seen before continuing along the path. The shadows had deepened and he walked more cautiously now, jumping at every rustle in the reeds or ripple in the water. It was only a short distance farther to the parish of St. Cross. As Jago rounded a bend near an old, crippled willow the reed beds gave way to a wide expanse of pasture, dotted with grazing cows. On the far side of the meadow the solid mass of the church rose above a long ribbon of wall beyond which he could also see a row of tall smoking chimneys and a square stone tower built over an arched gateway.

In order to reach the church Jago was going to have to cross the meadow, which meant that he would be clearly visible from any tree, gate or window on the far side. The cows offered his only chance of cover so Jago strolled out among them as casually as he could, slapping their rumps as he imagined a bored young farmhand might. The cows had been recently milked and shifted complacently as he made his way through. Nevertheless, he felt uncomfortably exposed.

Jago reached the wall and followed it around until he came to a wide gravel path that passed beneath an archway. A small printed sign screwed into the wall read TOURS OF THE ANCIENT FOUNDATION OF THE HOSPITAL OF ST. CROSS AND THE FOUNDATION OF THE ALMSHOUSE OF NOBLE POVERTY. Jago smiled wryly at the idea of "noble poverty." He had never seen anything noble about being poor. Still, if people wanted to pay a few pennies to look at it, then that was their business.

He peered along the path, which passed beneath another, more imposing arch before opening out into a little green with the church on the far side. St. Cross wasn't just a church; it was an ancient community of almshouses, cloisters and halls. Jago didn't have time to play the curious tourist, however, for at that moment the church doors opened. Evensong had finished.

According to the clock on the church tower, it was nearly seven o'clock as the worshippers stepped out of the gloom and into the early evening sun. Small knots of people gathered on the gravel, taking the time to chat in the golden light.

Jago walked quickly beneath the archways and ducked under the low porch of the gatekeeper's door, where he scrutinized the faces of the congregation from the safety of its shadows. Armbruster, he observed, was not among them. Was his quarry Piggott nearby, or Anna, the writer of the note? He bit his lip as he realized he didn't know who he was looking for, or why. He had almost made up his mind to nip back under the archway and loiter for a bit in the lane when, from somewhere to the side of him, he overheard a snatch of conversation.

"Anna, I have a small errand for you. . . ."

The speaker was a woman. Her voice was well educated, genteel. Jago's eyes scanned the groups of parishioners, searching for its owner. Could she have been talking to the same Anna who wrote the note in the watch?

"This basket—take it around to the back of the church, please, and leave it by the gate. It is just some old clothes for the poor."

"Of course, Miss Piggott."

There they were, just a few feet away from him. A tall, elegant woman dressed in ruched black silk and a hat with a delicate veil, and a younger girl, only fifteen or sixteen perhaps, in blue muslin. The girl was clearly a servant. Miss Piggott turned to speak to the chaplain while Anna took the basket and walked away.

In order to reach the back gate, Anna had to walk out beneath the stone archways and follow the wall around into the meadows that lay behind. Jago stepped out after her, and his boots crunched noisily on the gravel, but she did not look back. She moved decisively, confidently, as though she had nothing to fear. Was it Piggott she was hoping to meet? What did she know about Armbruster?

The shadows stretched out across the grass toward the river. The path was deserted and the air was completely still so when Jago came up behind her and touched her arm, she cried out, startled.

"Please, I need to ask you something . . . ," began Jago. He hadn't thought about what he was actually going to say. Anna stepped back. Her dark eyes narrowed warily as she weighed up his ragged trousers and grimy face.

"If you want charity, go to the church gate. I've nothing for you."

"No, no . . . I wanted to warn you—about Armbruster. . . ."

"Armbruster!" She drew the basket up in front of her chest as though trying to protect herself. "I don't know anyone . . ."

But Jago caught the flash of recognition in her voice. She knew Armbruster all right. He didn't have much time for lies. Callow had always been too full of them.

"He's been threatening me, and I can see that you know him."

"You must be mistaking me for someone else. . . ." she faltered.

"I don't think so," pressed Jago, nervous and impatient to move away from the open meadow. "He doesn't seem to be a friend of—"

"*Friend?*" Anna spat out the word. But then she stopped. She now had her back to the old flint wall. Her skirts brushed the ivy that clung to the stone. Something, however, had distracted her. She wasn't looking at Jago, but over his shoulder, down toward the river. Her eyes were wide, suddenly. Wide with fright.

"You've brought him with you," was all she said.

Jago swung round. He didn't see anything at first, but then, from out of the shade beneath an old horse chestnut tree, stepped three men. Two of them were dressed in workingmen's clothes and heavy, hobnailed boots. They each grasped an iron bar. The third man was Armbruster.

"You lying scum!" he snarled. "What are you doing here? Warned Piggott, have you? You'll pay for opening your big mouths, the pair of you!"

Armbruster moved closer. The two thugs with him spread out to cut off any possible escape route.

Jago stepped back. He felt the jagged flint of the wall digging into his shoulders and could hear Anna breathing rapidly beside him. There was nowhere to hide. The three men were slowly closing in. Armbruster's stare was fixed, unblinking. He was only a few feet away and Jago could see the corrugated skin of the scar beneath his eye.

"I said I'd kill you if you lied. I'm not a man who ever goes back on his word," he hissed, beckoning the other men to come closer.

Jago knew he had only one chance. He had learned, during his long and painful apprenticeship, about the art of surprise. It wasn't one of Callow's skills. Callow had never been subtle enough. Yet for Jago, offering the unexpected had become a matter of survival. Conjure up a distraction. Divert your audience's attention. Create the illusion of strength.

A clump of nettles reached almost to his left shoulder.

Jago grabbed a handful of stalks and, twisting around, thrust them straight into Armbruster's face. It wasn't enough to hurt him badly but Armbruster lifted his hands to his head as the stinging began and in that split second Jago took hold of Anna's hand and ran.

"Go after them!" screamed Armbruster, livid with rage as a rash of white bumps broke out across his flushed face. The two men set off with Armbruster not far behind, but Jago had the advantage now. He skirted back around the wall, away from the dangerous isolation of the riverbank. The churchgoers had all dispersed and the path leading up to the main road was empty. Running up that way would leave them too exposed so Jago pulled Anna into a narrow little lane on the right.

"He's following us!" cried Anna. Jago could hear boots thundering along behind them. "I can't keep up with you! Let go of my hand!" But Jago didn't let go. Anna's bonnet was getting in the way and she pushed it back behind her head, stumbling over a cart track as she did so. Jago yanked her up, pulling her along, forcing her to run.

On the left was a row of low flint and brick cottages. As Jago and Anna approached, two little girls in brown pinafores came out through one of the front gates and skipped toward the crossroads at the end of the lane where they stopped and turned to watch the figures hurtling toward them. Anna's breath came in short, sharp gasps. Jago could probably outrun their pursuers but Anna wore long skirts and a corset that squeezed her lungs. She wouldn't stand a chance on the open road that lay ahead. They needed to find somewhere to hide.

A low wall bordered the lane to the right. As they

turned the corner, Jago stopped and made a stirrup with his hands.

"Climb over, now!" He winced as she stepped on his fingers but somehow he managed to push her up and across the top of the wall before scrambling over himself. They landed in a heap on the other side and huddled there, trying not to breathe too loudly. Anna was shaking. They could hear their pursuers' footsteps slowing down.

"Where did they go?" puzzled one of the men. "Did they nip over the wall?"

Anna gripped Jago's arm, waiting to be discovered.

"Those two brats up there must have seen them." Now it was Armbruster speaking.

"Hey, you two! Did you see two people running? Where did they go?"

"We saw them. . . ." The little girl's voice was hesitant. What did these three strangers want her to say?

"Which way, damn you!" Armbruster was shouting at the children, but Jago had suddenly remembered the cricket ball in his pocket. Misdirection was the conjuror's mark. He knelt up, and with one swift movement threw the ball out across the wall. It bounced noisily into the narrow path that led back down to the river.

"Was it that way?" pressed Armbruster. The children must have nodded, for in an instant three sets of boots began to thunder off in the direction of Jago's ball. They had gone.

Jago's heart was pounding and his head was spinning. He leaned back against the wall and closed his eyes. But not for long, for Anna twisted around and slapped him, hard, across his face.

5

Anna's Story

"How *dare* you call me that man's friend!" Anna got to her feet and glared resentfully down at Jago. "How *dare* you drag me into your horrible dealings and involve me in whatever crime he seems to want to punish you for!"

Jago stood up slowly. He wasn't used to being hit by a girl.

"I never said Armbruster was your friend. But you know him. . . ."

"I don't want anything else to do with you. Go away."

Jago didn't know whether to laugh or hit her back. Hadn't he just risked his own skin to help her? He could have run twice as fast if he hadn't waited for her. She might be two or three years older, but older people, to Jago's mind, often found it convenient to forget about fairness.

"I'm not going anywhere. That man wanted to shut both of us up and I want to know why."

Anna stood still. Her eyes followed the path that ran down toward the river, checking that the three men really had gone.

"He's an evil man. . . ."

Jago could see that she still felt afraid. He realized he would have to be patient if he wanted her to talk.

"Look," he said gently. "We should get away from here, in case they come back."

"My mistress is expecting me. I dropped her basket

somewhere. . . ." Anna's anger had gone. She was unsure now.

"Then why don't I walk with you? I'll see you home safely and you can tell me what you know." But as soon as he said it, Jago knew he had gone too far.

"You? You're just some street boy. Why should I tell you anything?"

Jago put out his hand to help her over the wall.

"And you're some fine lady's maid who wasn't really running for her life a few minutes ago? He knew you! You know him!"

Once more he had said too much. She turned on him and he thought for a moment that she was about to slap him again. Perhaps it was better not to reveal that he had overheard her conversation in the graveyard the night before.

"Look," he said quietly. "He's seen us together. So he thinks we're involved together. Now the way I see it, you've brought me into this mess, not the other way around." Jago was bluffing, but it seemed his only option. "He wanted to kill me because I was with you. So you'd better start telling me what you know about this Mr. Armbruster."

Anna sighed and began to walk up the lane in the direction of the main road.

"I live this way."

As Jago walked beside her, she began to tell her story.

"I work in a big house out along the Southampton Road. My mistress is Miss Catherine Piggott. I've been her lady's maid for over two years now. She's a wonderful lady, so kind and considerate. She's taught me to read, she gives me her old clothes and she works tirelessly to raise funds for the poorhouse. She gives her time to so many good causes. . . ."

"She sounds very kind," said Jago.

"Yes . . . yes. Well, you see, she had a dear father, old Mr. Piggott. But poor Mr. Piggott died two months ago. He was a very wealthy man. People said his fortune came from the South American slave trade. He built a great new house, gave his children everything they needed. . . . He bought the old brewery in town, renamed it Paradise Ales and built it up into a fine concern. Then a few months before he died, he sold the business. Against all advice he invested the profits in a South American scheme to build sewers in Rio de Janeiro." Anna shook her head disbelievingly. "Who cares if some faraway place in South America doesn't smell nice? They can't even build us proper sewers in Winchester! Anyway, the investment scheme was nothing but a hoax and Mr. Piggott lost all his money. The shock brought on his illness. Miss Piggott had his affairs to attend to so I spent the next few weeks looking after him but he died anyway. His solicitor read the will last week. Fortunately the house was not affected and was left to Miss Piggott, along with a small annual income for her personal use. But her brother, Mr. Robert Piggott, was left 'the sum total of all remaining monies, stocks and bonds.' Nothing, in other words."

Anna and Jago had reached the main road. Jago looked carefully for any sign of Armbruster and his men, but all was quiet. A horse-drawn hay wagon swayed slowly toward town, and a couple of children hung around the doorway of the inn on the corner, but it was evening now and most of the day's traffic had passed. To the right ran Front Street with its low cottages and village shop. The spires and rooftops of Winchester lay beyond. To the left, the buildings petered out as Front Street became the turnpike that followed the river all the way to Southampton and the sea.

"This way," pointed Anna, crossing over and turning left, away from the town. "Mr. Robert—he'd had big expectations, you see. He couldn't understand why his father hadn't simply handed the brewery over to him. He found it difficult to forgive his father for investing so foolishly, without first seeking advice."

"He must have felt that pretty badly . . . ," murmured Jago, by way of encouragement.

"It was a bitter blow, yes. Mr. Robert worked hard for his father for many years, and he has ended up with nothing. Of course Miss Piggott has offered him a home with her, but he's too proud. Things have been difficult between them since Mr. Piggott died. . . ." Anna hesitated. The conversation was clearly a painful one. "I . . . I took some things I shouldn't have taken and gave them to Mr. Robert. Mr. Piggott meant them for his son, I'm sure, but now Mr. Robert says he's off to Brazil. . . ." She put her hands to her face and moaned softly. "What have I done?"

Jago scratched his nose. So Robert Piggott was the man she had met at the cathedral the night before. But he didn't think she'd said anything yet that deserved his sympathy.

"I still don't see what all this has to do with Armbruster."

"No. Well, Mr. Armbruster was the agent appointed by Mr. Piggott to oversee his financial affairs. He swears he warned against any investment in South America, but that the old master was blinded by the figures and refused to take his advice. I . . . I don't believe him though. I think he's lying."

"Why?" asked Jago, though he was more than ready to believe it.

"Well, I haven't got any proof, but a few weeks ago I found an envelope addressed to Mr. Armbruster lying half-burnt in the grate of the room he used as his office. The postmark was from Brazil. As I picked it up to look at the unusual handwriting Mr. Armbruster walked up behind me and snatched it out of my hand. I suppose it might have been some perfectly harmless correspondence, but the postal date was September 1873—before Mr. Piggott had even heard of the sewer scheme. Anyway, Mr. Armbruster was furious with me for touching something that belonged to him. That evening he emptied his desk of every single scrap of paper, and then he left the house and the family's employ. I never saw the envelope again and he never mentioned it afterward, but lately I'm sure he's been following me and now, after what has happened today, I've no doubt of his guilt."

"Have you told Piggott, or your mistress, any of this?"

"I have tried to tell Mr. Robert, yes, but I have no proof. He is so disturbed by events that he has begun to believe that his father deliberately deprived him of his inheritance. Anyway, he is determined to seek the truth in South America. He leaves the country in a day or two, and just as well if that horrible man is out looking for him. Miss Catherine Piggott I will never tell. She trusted her father's judgment and I couldn't bear to see her troubled any further." Anna lowered her head, but not before Jago saw the hesitant flicker in her eyes.

"But that doesn't seem right! Surely Miss Piggott would want to see justice done?"

"No!" Anna shouted the word. She pressed her knuckles into her temple as though trying by sheer physical pressure to regain her self-control. "No. It is more . . . complicated. There has to be another way." She plucked off a tight, unripe blackberry from the bramble in the hedge beside her. "Do you believe it is possible to speak with the dead?"

"What? You mean séances, spirits and all that mystical hocus-pocus?" Jago smiled, but Anna looked hurt.

"Mr. Robert needs to find out what has been going on. If he could communicate with old Mr. Piggott . . . ask him whether Mr. Armbruster persuaded him to part with his money . . ."

"Those mediums in town are just frauds," said Jago, as kindly as he could. "Don't waste your money. Believe me, I know."

They had stopped in front of a large flint and brick mansion, newly built, set well back from the road in neatly laid out grounds. A nameplate screwed to the wrought iron gates announced FLINTLOCK GRANGE. It looked as though it was the last house out in that direction for several miles. A horse chestnut tree threw its long shadow across the clipped lawn.

Anna sighed, as though she felt she had said too much.

"This is Miss Piggott's house. I must go now."

"Aren't you worried that Armbruster will come looking for you again?"

"No. He won't come here. My mistress despises him—she won't let him through the gates."

She seemed very sure all of a sudden. "I have to go now. Good-bye."

Jago was curious to know more about Armbruster, but Anna clearly didn't want to stand there with him any longer. He turned and set off down the road toward the town. After a few steps, however, he stopped and looked back. The Piggott house was set at the end of a long gravel drive, yet Anna was nowhere to be seen. She must have cut across the lawn and, despite her corset, been running very fast indeed.

The late sun was beginning its descent behind the trees. Jago put his hands in his pockets, thrust his bony shoulders forward and walked at a brisk pace. It had seemed unwise to mention the fact that he had read the note in the watch, but now that he had time to think, he realized that there was plenty he still didn't understand.

Anna hadn't mentioned the note. She hadn't said anything about meeting Mr. Robert after evensong. Armbruster, however, did know about the note. Perhaps he had actually written it. He had clearly gone to St. Cross in order to set upon Mr. Robert and kill him.

So where did this leave Anna? Was she as innocent as she appeared? Her fear of Armbruster seemed genuine enough, but how had Armbruster managed to plant the note in the watch if he wasn't allowed to come near

Flintlock Grange? Anna hadn't mentioned the key she had taken, either. Keys were for secrets. Anna was hiding something—of that much Jago was certain.

Armbruster was a more predictable type of fellow. He was a crook, a bully and now a potential murderer. Simple. The best thing that Jago could do was, like Anna, stay out of his way. And that would be easy enough, for he and Callow were due to pack up and head out for Stockbridge the next day.

"You idiot!" groaned Jago, slapping his forehead with the palm of his hand. He had completely forgotten the early start that they were supposed to be making in the morning. If Callow had woken already he'd be in a foul mood, made worse if Jago wasn't there to pack up the cart and find him some food.

Jago began to run along the road. It wasn't much farther back to Middle Brook Street. If he wasn't quick he was sure to get a beating when he arrived at Mrs. Tyle's, and in his haste he pushed his growing unease to the back of his mind.

It was nearly nine o'clock by the time he turned into the gloomy warren of alleys and tenements known as the Brooks. The warm evening air gave the stench from the trickling stream that served as the local sewer an added pungency. Mrs. Tyle's Threepenny Lodging House was one of the older buildings, a half-timbered, trussed-up place, black with age and misery. No one stayed there unless things were pretty bad. Jago turned into the shadowy yard and approached the back door. Mrs. Tyle was still sitting there, still smoking her pipe. It looked as though she hadn't moved for hours.

"Is he awake yet?" asked Jago, pushing open the battered door.

"I s'pose he must be." The old woman blew out a gray cloud of smoke. "He's had visitors."

Jago entered the darkened building. Gaslight was still a novelty in this part of town and it was no use asking Mrs. Tyle for a candle. He felt his way along the dank wall of the corridor toward the front room. A box or crate lay in his path and he tripped over it, noisily. Callow didn't like him crashing about. Yet it wasn't his uncle's curses that greeted him at the doorway. All Jago could hear was someone's labored breathing until the stale air shuddered with the sound of a long, agonized groan.

6
Left for Dead

It took forever for Jago to find a candle and a match and struggle over the upturned furniture to where Callow lay. There was blood everywhere. It was still trickling out of a large gash across the old man's forehead. The mattress was soaked and scarlet splashes stained the peeling wall behind him. But he wasn't dead.

"What happened?" whispered Jago as he tried to haul Callow up into a sitting position.

"Get off me! Aaah!" Callow yelped as Jago leaned him back against the wall and stuffed his tattered jacket behind the old man's head. "Where the 'ell 'ave you been?"

"Nowhere," replied Jago. "I'll go and ask Mrs. Tyle for a basin of water."

"It's not water I need, it's bleedin' gin!" gasped Callow. "The old bag'll 'ave a bottle or two stashed away somewhere. Go and tell her I'll owe her."

Mrs. Tyle, however, wasn't about to let Callow have anything else on credit.

"Not likely!" she muttered as she shuffled along the hall to the front room. "And I won't 'ave fights in my 'ouse! This is a respectable place and I don't want the Law sniffing around after trouble—I've got one of me gatherings in 'ere tomorrow...." She kicked a broken chair out of her way and bent down to inspect Callow's mattress. "You'd better be going to pay for this lot! This was me best front parlor! It was me only parlor!"

"Who did it?" asked Jago, ignoring Mrs. Tyle.

"Who did it? I'll tell you who did it . . . a couple of bums sent by that knuckle-crunching chum of yours from the pub, that's who!" Callow coughed and spat out a broken tooth. "Friendly bugger, wasn't he? Those council fellers think they can throw their weight around, beat up who they like, and because we're all 'ardly scraping an honest living together ourselves, we can't touch 'em!"

Callow was right. There was nothing they could do to stop the likes of Armbruster. Not when he could get them hauled off to jail with a wave of his hand. Jago had a sick feeling in the pit of his stomach. What had he gone and done? If only he hadn't found the stupid watch in the first place. Armbruster didn't know how much he knew, but he'd seen him with Anna. Clearly he wasn't about to let Jago get away.

"They thought they was leaving me for dead, didn't they?" continued Callow. "But I tell you what, young Stonecipher—they was after *you*. I 'eard 'em." He winced as he tried to sit up. "So I don't want you around me no more. You're trouble and I've 'ad enough of yer. Just toddle off and don't come back."

It wasn't the first time that Callow had told Jago to get lost. When he was drunk he was always pushing him away and Jago knew to keep out of sight until the old man sobered up and wanted someone to yell at again. This time, however, Jago chose to take him at his word. He was already a far better conjuror than Callow, even if

Callow refused to believe it. Jago had nothing more to learn from him. The only thing that bound him to his uncle was a shared relative, now dead. Hadn't Callow been ready to hand him over to Armbruster in the pub that morning? Not only that, but Armbruster's men had known exactly where to find Callow. And they would almost certainly return for Jago.

"Don't worry, I'm off!" he muttered, turning toward the door. Yet something made him pause in the hallway. "You should get away from here, Uncle. If they come back for me, they'll find you still here."

"Oh, he'll be gone by morning all right!" shouted Mrs. Tyle. "I don't want him 'ere, though I'll see I get me damages for this lot first!"

"I can't get up," mumbled Callow, but Mrs. Tyle wasn't going to be put off.

"Don't be such a boneless old dizzard!" she scolded. "Head wounds always make a great bloody mess, but they're never as bad as they look. You've paid for the night but you're out by morning!"

So Jago left the house and walked out into the dusk. He had nowhere to go of course, but he knew two things. First, Armbruster's men would be out looking for him. Second, he hadn't eaten since early morning and his stomach was complaining, loudly.

Middle Brook Street didn't have much to offer in the way of dinner. There were a couple of sooty pubs but the drinkers inside were too hard or too desperate to show any mercy to a young pickpocket if he got himself caught.

"Lookin' for trouble?"

A young woman, two children balanced on her hips, eyed Jago suspiciously from a doorway.

"You're not from around 'ere, are yer?" One of her children was grumbling softly. She wiped its nose with her apron. "Go on, then!"

Her voice wasn't unkind, but Jago knew that this neighborhood would only protect its own. Where could he hide? He hopped over the trickling ditch that sliced the road in half and headed toward the center of town. No one would notice a stranger in the High Street—not if he didn't attract attention to himself. And no one was better than Jago Stonecipher at melting into a crowd.

Night was falling as Jago left the grimy tenements behind him. Most shops had long since shut up for the day, but the High Street was still doing a brisk trade. Matches, hot coffee, flowers, tobacco—hawkers flogged their goods from every street corner. Men and women flowed in and out of the inns and pubs in steady streams, laughing, shouting, sometimes fighting. Light spilled across the street from crowded doorways and brightly lit windows. Jago slowed down, sticking to the shadows. Outside the Black Swan a woman staggered and bumped into him.

"Ooh, good job you was there, or I'd be in the gutter by now!" she laughed. Jago allowed himself a brief smile. This was his kind of crowd. Country people in town for the summer fair, having a good time, not afraid of strangers.

From the kitchen of the Black Swan came the rich thick smell of dumplings and gravy. Jago's hunger returned with a stab. He didn't want a half-cold pie, stolen on the run. He wanted a hot beef dinner with all the trimmings. The trouble was, getting it would mean drawing attention to himself. He peered through the greasy windows. The bar was packed but there was no sign of Armbruster or his thugs. Jago decided to risk it.

The Black Swan was a coaching inn. It catered to better-off travelers as well as the usual Saturday night drinkers. Hot meals were served in the low-beamed dining room at the back, where ladies and gentlemen could rest with a little more privacy than was possible in the main bar. Jago walked quickly through the double doors and followed the sounds of clinking cutlery down the stone-flagged passage that led to the back room. High-backed wooden benches divided the space up into little cubicles for the comfort of the diners. Most of the seats were occupied, and the tables in front of them were laden with steaming soup tureens and platters of beef. The heady fog of beery breath and boiling vegetables made Jago's mouth water.

Jago knew he would have to work quickly. He approached a table where a respectably dressed man sat eating steak and kidney pie with his wife and two children.

"Good evening!" he began, politely. The family looked up, surprised.

"Would your children like to see a magic trick?"

"No," grunted the father. "Clear off or I'll call the landlord."

The man began to wave to the barman by the door. Jago moved away quickly.

At the next table, two girls sat finishing plates of soup. They looked like sisters. They were dressed in traveling cloaks and whispered excitedly to one another as they ate.

"Good evening, ladies!"

"Go away!" said the older of the pair, not more than sixteen but quite the young lady in her grown-up clothes. The younger one was laughing a little, looking up at him with bright, inquisitive eyes. She and her sister were obviously enjoying their evening without a chaperone.

Jago took his chance. He picked up a glass of water and held it in his right hand. Then he took a handkerchief from his pocket and used it to pick up a penny that had been left on the table as a tip.

"That's not yours!" exclaimed the older girl, but Jago put his finger to his lips and smiled and she shut up, curious to see what he would do next.

Covering the glass with the handkerchief and gripping the coin through the cloth, Jago dropped the penny. The sisters heard it clink as it fell into the glass. Jago lifted the cloth and revealed the penny sitting in the bottom of the glass. Then he replaced the cloth and a moment later removed it again. This time the coin had completely disappeared.

"How did you do that?" asked the younger girl. "Go on, show us! We'll let you keep the penny, won't we, Maud?"

It seemed like a fair deal to Jago. He showed them how he covered the glass, tilting it under the cloth so that when he dropped the penny it clinked against the outside and slid down into his waiting right hand. The glass was then revealed with the penny held underneath, though from above it looked as though the coin was actually sitting in the water at the bottom. When the glass was covered again, Jago removed his right hand with the coin, and the glass appeared empty. It was a simple trick, but Jago was well practiced and the sisters were impressed.

"Show us some more! Please!"

The landlord, however, had noticed Jago standing at the table.

"Are you pestering my customers? Go on! Clear off before I kick you out!" Jago winced as his arm was twisted in the landlord's hairy fist.

"No! Don't be hard on him! He was entertaining us, and very well too!"

"Look, misses, he's a scruffy little pickpocket after whatever he can get. What would your mama say?"

"She's resting upstairs. Maud's in charge. If we buy him his dinner, you won't object to his staying, will you?" The younger girl was keen to see a few more of Jago's tricks. There wasn't much else to divert them on their long and tedious journey.

"It's your money," grumbled the landlord as he turned away.

So Jago got his hot beef dinner. The girls giggled at the way he bent over his food, shoveling it into his mouth. He'd earned it though and didn't mind. The younger sister reminded Jago of Clara. He had never known his parents, but Clara had taken care of him and it was still her bubbling laughter that calmed him through his restless dreams.

When Jago had finished his second helping of dumplings and gravy, the sisters wished him good night, paid the bill and left to inquire after the whereabouts of their coach. Most of the other diners had similarly departed, and Jago had no choice but to leave the inn himself. It was after midnight and he was back where he'd started—on the street. The High Street hostelries were beginning to close their doors and the drinkers crawling out of the pubs now seemed less friendly, more unpredictable.

Jago paused in the doorway of the Black Swan, hesitant for the first time that day. He looked up. There was no moon. The stars were hidden behind the heavy blanket of night and the weight of exhaustion began to overwhelm him. He squatted down on the pavement for a moment, undecided about where to go next. Returning to Callow was out of the question, but it felt strange nevertheless to be alone and for no one to tell him where he was to spend the night.

"Get out of my way!"

A tall, dark figure emerged from the doorway behind Jago, pushing past him and marching off down the road. It wasn't Armbruster, but it might have been. Jago found himself shaking.

He got to his feet, took a deep breath and began to walk away from the town, up the West Hill toward the prison. Somewhere along the road, hidden in the midnight shadows, he curled up and went to sleep, too tired to shiver and reach for the jacket he'd left in Middle Brook Street under Callow's battered head.

7

Flintlock Grange

Jago crouched in the dense shade of a yew tree and watched the house. He hadn't come through the wrought-iron gates; he had scrambled over the ivy-clad wall. Flintlock Grange looked welcoming enough in the bright morning sunshine, but the warmth didn't penetrate the gloom beneath the trees and his clothes were still damp with the dew that had drenched him in the night.

The house had an imposing pillared porch, flanked by tall bay windows on either side. A neat box hedge had been planted beneath the windows and yellow roses grew beside the steps. Everything was ordered, tidy, bright. The sunlight glanced off the polished window-panes, and the heavy brass door knocker shone. A substantial house, reflecting the life of a substantial man. Paradise Ales had been a profitable business, in its time. Jago wondered how Anna's mistress would be able to maintain it now that the money was gone. Perhaps the place would be put up for sale.

As Jago watched, a man in a cloth cap with a large wicker basket over each arm walked through the gate and made his way up the curve of the drive. His feet crunched loudly on the gravel. A footpath wound around the side of the house and the man followed it to a plain green-painted door. The tradesmen's entrance. He knocked and almost immediately the door opened. A woman appeared and looked anxiously back down the drive. It was Anna. Then she took the man's arm and pulled him inside. The door was shut behind them.

Jago shifted uncomfortably in the undergrowth. His legs were beginning to ache from crouching down for so long. He knew that it was probably a mistake to be there at all. Now that Callow had dismissed him, Jago was a free agent, if ever a lad on the streets could be called such a thing. He could walk to Southampton in a day and leave all this playing with fire behind him. A busy port like Southampton was the perfect place in which to forget the past and become somebody new—somebody who wasn't tarred with Callow's brush, who didn't steal but instead made his way in the world by talent, by ingenuity and by simple hard graft. Surely Armbruster would never trace him there?

Yet when Jago had woken that morning, stiff with cold and damp, his vague unease about Anna and her story had not gone away. "Curiosity killed the cat" he could hear Callow muttering, but Callow was the one who had been left for dead the day before. Something about Anna didn't add up. Why was a lady's maid opening the door to tradesmen? Surely that was the scullery maid's job? It was almost as if Anna had been watching out for the man.

Just then the green side door reopened and the butcher or baker, or whoever he was, stepped back out into the sunshine. He hurried down the drive, his cap pulled down low as if to shade his face—yet he had an oddly familiar hunch to his shoulders. Then he was gone.

Jago decided to take his chance. He stood up painfully and waited a moment for the blood to return to his legs.

Then with a quick glance up at the windows of the house, he darted out of the undergrowth and cut across the grass. He didn't want anyone to hear his footsteps approaching on the gravel. Skirting around the side of the house, he stopped in front of the closed side door and tapped softly with his fingers. No reply. He knocked a little louder. This time he could hear footsteps and a bolt being drawn back. The door opened a crack. Jago could see no one in the small wedge of darkness beyond.

"Who is it?" a woman's voice asked nervously.

"I want to see Anna."

"Please go away."

The door began to shut, but Jago blocked it with his foot.

"Anna, it's me. Jago. From last night."

"What do you want?" The door didn't open any farther, but Anna's white face peered out through the gap.

"I want to talk to you."

"Talk? Why?"

"Because I reckon you've been telling a taradiddle or two! How much does your mistress know about Armbruster? You said she won't have anything to do with him, so she must have suspicions of her own. No magistrate'll believe a scraggy little shaver like me, but there's nothing to stop her going to the police. He's out looking for me! Neither of us are safe!"

"Keep your voice down. I don't want her to be worried by any of this."

"All right—maybe I should tell her that you're having some sort of secret carry-on with her brother? That was him who came to the house just now, wasn't it?"

"No!"

Jago leaned against the door, determined that she wouldn't be able to close it without first considering what he had to say.

"Anna, we've got to help each other! Armbruster's thugs laid into my uncle last night. Don't pretend you haven't spoken to Piggott—what did he have to say?"

Anna didn't answer. Instead she gave the door a shove, almost jamming Jago's fingers in the frame.

"Do you want me to bang on the front door and yell for Miss Piggott myself? How would that help?" Jago didn't want to threaten her—he'd suffered Callow's bullying long enough to know how terrible it felt. All the same, it seemed to him that she simply didn't understand the danger they were in. Scaring her seemed to be the only way to get her to listen. "She'd probably throw you out if she found out, wouldn't she? Her maid and her brother! A bit odd I reckon—she's not exactly going to give you her blessing!"

He heard a stifled sob from behind the door.

"Miss Piggott is still grieving! She doesn't need any more trouble." Anna's tone was pleading now. "Please, just leave us alone."

But it was too late. From somewhere behind Anna came the sound of voices.

"Is that the butcher, Anna? Cook here was just telling me about a mistake with last week's order."

"Miss Piggott!" Anna tried once more to shut the door, but Jago's foot was still wedged in the gap.

"Oh, let me speak to him. I'm sure he can do better than the gristly beef we have been tolerating lately."

The door was opened suddenly, so that Jago nearly fell across the threshold.

"Well, you're not the butcher!" exclaimed a floury-fisted woman in a large apron.

"No indeed, Cook!" Miss Piggott stepped forward, laughing softly. "Anna, a friend of yours, I expect?"

"Miss Piggott, I . . ."

Anna was all confusion, but Jago quickly improvised.

"I'm Jago Stonecipher, parlor magician, madam. I was wondering, if you'll pardon my presumption, whether there are any young ones of the house with a birthday around the corner? I'm a skillful hand at children's parties. . . ."

Jago took off his cap and waited politely.

"Well, Mr. Stonecipher, do you not think that you are a little young to be offering your services around the neighborhood?" Catherine Piggott smiled, her eyes full of dry amusement.

"Not at all, madam! I have served a long apprentice-ship and I reckon I know a fair bit about the magician's craft. Let me show you. . . ."

Jago bent down and picked a small daisy from the lawn's edge behind him. He quickly plucked its petals and then, before Anna could protest, he stepped forward and threw them over her hair.

"From daisy showers come hothouse flowers!"

Quick as lightning he reached behind her and produced a bunch of yellow roses tied with glossy strands of ivy.

Anna shook away the daisy petals, flushed and angry. Miss Piggott, however, was clearly delighted.

"Bravo, young man! Very pretty, even though the roses

are rather familiar. . . ." Her laughter was soft and low. "I should like to see more of your magic! Come inside—you must tell me where you learned such tricks. . . ."

The kitchen was dark and cool. Miss Piggott led the way around a scrubbed pine table and out into the passageway beyond. She glided smoothly in her elaborately gathered bustle and narrow skirts, as if her fashionable clothes did not impede her. Jago followed her past tall dressers full of painted china, dim doorways, larders and linen cupboards. He had never been inside such a fine house before. At the end of the passage they stepped out into the main hall. Jago would have liked to stop and gaze upward, let his eyes linger on the curved mahogany staircase, the stained glass windows, the paintings and the crystal chandelier, but Anna gave him a push from behind and on he walked, his heavy boots thudding across the smooth chestnut parquet.

"Let's take our guest into the morning room, Anna. We shall be comfortable in there." Miss Piggott beckoned to Jago as Anna held open the door.

The morning room was dominated by a pair of tall bay windows. Sunshine streamed past moss green velvet curtains and spilled across the crimson-colored rug. Miss Piggott sat down on a low sofa with her back to the light, silhouetted against the bright glare from behind. Jago stood in the middle of the room and gazed at the polished furniture, the vases of flowers and the marble mantelpiece with its artful display of porcelain figurines.

"So tell me, Mr. Stonecipher, where did you learn to speak so nicely?" Jago couldn't see her face without squinting, but her voice seemed kind, if gently teasing.

Anna, standing quietly beside the sofa, clearly trusted her. Jago had never trusted anyone—not since his sister's death. Yet Catherine Piggott was possibly the only person who could put a stop to Armbruster. Anna said her mistress hated him—wouldn't let him into the house. Well, she must have her reasons. Telling her about Callow would do no harm, and might provoke her into taking action against Armbruster. He took a deep breath.

"My parents died when I was a baby. My sister took care of me—Clara, she was called. She was clever. She scraped a living as a printer's runner and wrote letters for people on the docks at Portsmouth. She found me books and taught me to read. She wanted me to make something of myself."

Jago closed his eyes for a moment. He could hear his sister's voice inside his head, telling him about the power of words and teaching him to unlock their secrets. Yet Clara's dreams had so far brought him nothing. Reading the note in the watch had only landed him in trouble. He banished the memories from his mind and opened his eyes.

"Anyway, she died. My uncle, a showman by the name of Archibald Callow, took me on as his apprentice, but mostly I've taught myself."

"I see. Your sister's death must have been a great loss to you." Miss Piggott leaned across and touched Anna lightly on the arm. "Would you please ask Dolly to bring coffee?"

Anna bobbed a little curtsy and walked toward the door. She glanced nervously at Jago on her way out, but he didn't catch her eye. Miss Piggott was addressing him again.

"So your uncle—he took care of you?"

Jago saw little point in mentioning the beatings, the hunger when Callow was off boozing, the way he had been strapped into the pony harness and forced to pull the props cart when the poor animal had finally died of exhaustion. . . .

"No, he didn't take care of me. I take care of myself. Or at least, I managed just fine until Armbruster came along."

"Armbruster? Mr. Armbruster?" Miss Piggott sat forward, but her voice was calm. "What do you know of him?"

"He almost killed Callow. Not that I care, except that now he wants to kill me."

"I see. And you know, I take it, that Mr. Armbruster was formerly employed by my late father? Is that why you have come here?"

Jago took a step forward. He was still having difficulty in seeing Miss Piggott clearly—her face was a shadow against the bright glare of the sunlight.

"I've heard rumors. That maybe Armbruster stole your family's money. That you and he aren't exactly friends. I just thought that . . . maybe if you had suspicions about him, and I could prove that he hurt my uncle . . . the magistrate would listen to a fine lady like you."

Miss Piggott rose to her feet and walked slowly over to a locked walnut bureau. Her fingers brushed the polished surface as she picked up a small daguerreotype of an elderly man and gazed at it for a minute or two.

"You are very presumptuous, Mr. Stonecipher." She had her back to Jago. Perhaps he had made a mistake in thinking that she might be prepared to take his side against Armbruster.

He waited. The room was silent. Only the dust danced across the sunlit spaces.

"Coffee, ma'am."

Jago jumped a little as the kitchen maid suddenly appeared with a silver tray. Anna hovered in the doorway behind her. Miss Piggott put down the picture and turned around.

"Thank you, Dolly. Anna, please accompany Mr. Stonecipher back to the kitchens and ask Cook to find him some breakfast." She looked at Jago, her smooth, unlined face out of the shadows at last. "I may be able to help you, but I need to give some careful thought to the whole business—to consider my own position in this matter. Mr. Armbruster is a man of considerable influence in this city."

Miss Piggott's eyes were cool and gray. Jago found himself staring at her, lost for a second in the pull of her gaze. He was tired. His eyelids felt impossibly heavy. Now that he had unburdened himself he wanted nothing more than to lie down and go to sleep. Miss Piggott, however, was still speaking and he shook his head to clear away the torpor that had so strangely clouded his mind.

"Go and have something to eat. Then I should like to talk to you again." Her tone was decisive. Jago turned and left the room.

Out in the hall, Anna seized Jago's arm and pinched it, hard.

"Did you say anything to her about Mr. Robert? Tell me. . . ."

"No. No, I said nothing about either of you. Your

64

affair's got nothing to do with me—I just want Armbruster off my back."

Anna wasn't about to let the subject drop, however. She sat at the kitchen table and watched while he ate the eggs that Cook had grudgingly prepared for him.

"Did she mention Mr. Robert at all?"

Jago shook his head and reached out for another piece of bread and butter.

"Did she ask about me?"

"*No!*" He hadn't meant to shout, but he couldn't understand why Anna was so obstinately oblivious to the more immediate danger from Armbruster. Now all she seemed to care about was whether or not Miss Piggott knew about her relationship with Robert Piggott. Jago picked up the cup of milk in front of him and drank it down, playing for time. Was she still hiding something? Clearly Anna's view of her situation was skewed by her feelings for Mr. Robert. Part of him wanted to tell her that a man like Mr. Robert wasn't going to marry a lady's maid; that when he returned empty-handed from South America he would be looking to marry a woman with money now that he didn't have any. Yet Jago couldn't bring himself to crush her so heartlessly. She was entitled to her dreams, just like anyone. He put down his empty cup and this time spoke more gently.

"Why don't you tell Miss Piggott about Armbruster, and have him put away where he belongs? Then we'd all be able to sleep more easy and, you never know, Mr. Robert might even get his father's money back."

Anna's face was crumpling, her eyes filling with tears.

"I can't. You have no idea . . . You don't know what's at stake. . . ."

"What I know is that Armbruster tried to kill us."

"It's not that simple!"

"Why? Just tell me, Anna!"

Anna looked down and fiddled with a loose thread in the sleeve of her dress.

"Mr. Armbruster says he'll tell Miss Piggott about me and Mr. Robert, and he'll tell her that I took old Mr. Piggott's watch. Only to give to Mr. Robert though! But I'd lose my position. I've no family—I'd lose everything. You should never have interfered. I didn't ask you to interfere."

So that was his mistake. He had interfered. Never mind that his life had been threatened, or that he had saved Anna's skin in the meadows the day before. Jago scraped back his chair and stood up. He was beginning to see things more clearly now, on a full stomach.

Anna had a comfortable life with Miss Piggott. All the servants did. Eggs for breakfast, soft beds, reading lessons. No wonder Anna didn't want to risk any of this to get to the bottom of Armbruster's mischief. Miss Piggott wasn't going to help someone like him stop Armbruster either. It was Robert's money that had disappeared, not hers. She had her fine house, her fleet of servants, and it seemed there was no love lost between brother and sister. Perhaps Armbruster had actually done her a favor by cutting Robert out of the picture.

"I'm going. I can't help you and you won't help me. You can tell your Miss Piggott what you like. Tell her I'll manage well enough on my own. Always have done. . . ."

Anna grasped at his arm. "Don't go! I didn't mean to . . . She wants to see you, and it would look very bad if you went without speaking to her again!"

Yet Jago had made up his mind. He felt sorry for Anna, and for Miss Piggott too, in a way. They cared too much about what others might think. They both had a certain position in society and they weren't about to jeopardize any of that in order to see justice done.

Much better, Jago told himself, not to have a position in society. He was on the outside looking in, like a child pressing its eye to the window of a perfect little dolls' house and, finding it empty, running away to find a more interesting game to play. With a flick of his arm Jago shook himself free of Anna's grasp and made for the door, but before he stepped out into the sunlight, he paused for a moment.

"Just keep out of Armbruster's way, all right?"

Anna said nothing, yet Jago saw her shiver. She was still afraid.

8

The Rags in the Yard

Jago stopped to catch his breath at the bottom of the drive. To his left lay St. Cross, with the long gray roof of Winchester Cathedral grazing the skyline beyond. On his right the turnpike road stretched into the distance. It seemed as good a place as any to hitch a ride out of town. Southampton would do, or Portsmouth . . . anywhere just so long as Armbruster couldn't find him. He'd start over, for he, unlike Anna, knew how to survive in the real world.

It was going to be another hot day. Jago shielded his eyes with his hand and peered back along the road. A corn merchant's cart was trundling toward him, the poor horse in a lather from the heat and the flies. The driver looked half asleep. Jago reckoned he wouldn't be seen if he jumped up and hid between the bulky burlap sacks— he might even manage a bit of a nap.

It wasn't until the cart was nearly level with him, however, that Jago realized he had forgotten his jacket. Where had he left it? Suddenly the breakfast he'd just eaten churned sickeningly inside him. He had left his jacket under Callow's bloody head back at Mrs. Tyle's. The jacket itself didn't matter, of course, but Clara's letter-block did, tucked away in a hole in the hem. It was his only remaining connection to his past—or rather, the bits of his past that he cared to remember.

Jago stepped back and let the corn merchant's cart

pass by. Despite the sunshine, a wave of despondency rolled over him like a damp fog. So much for an easy ride to a brand-new life. He wondered bitterly if he'd ever really meant to escape. How could he have been stupid enough to leave anything so precious with Callow? There was only one thing to be done, and when the dust from the cart wheels had settled he turned around and trudged back along the road toward Winchester.

It was nearly eleven by the time he got back to Middle Brook Street. He had walked fast, choosing the river route and ducking into the reeds every time he heard someone approach. No one had seen him—or at least, no one had challenged him. Jago didn't feel safe though. A police constable had stared at him from under his tall black helmet as he rounded the corner of Colebrook Street and he could have sworn he'd seen one of Armbruster's thugs in the shadow of a tavern doorway. He felt almost relieved as he slipped into the furtive gloom of Mrs. Tyle's yard.

Mrs. Tyle was not at her usual vantage point on the steps. A bundle of rags lay where they had been dumped on the cobbles below and Jago had to climb over them to reach the back door. As he did so, however, he heard a faint whimper.

"Don't kick me . . . please . . . no more kicking . . ."

Jago leaped back in disgust, for the voice was unmistakable. Somewhere underneath the filthy heap lay Archibald Callow.

"What have you done with my jacket?" Jago demanded, not wanting to hang around a moment longer than he had to. Armbruster's men might, even now, be watching the building.

"Jago . . . Jago . . . is that you?" croaked the bundle. All Jago could see of Callow was his feet. He'd lost his boots somewhere and his scabby toes were mottled greenish purple. Jago pulled at the scrap of crumpled cloth that covered the old man's face and found that it was his jacket, barely recognizable now and caked in dried blood. But that was forgotten when he saw what lay beneath.

"Oh . . . God . . ." he stuttered, standing back in horror. Armbruster's men had been rather more thorough than Mrs. Tyle had given them credit for. Since the previous evening Callow's face had swollen to twice its usual size. The cut on his head was oozing wetly. He could barely open his bruised and blackened eyelids, and when Jago tried to sit him up, he cried out, shrieking like an animal.

"Don't . . . touch me . . . aargh!"

This was no amateurish performance. Callow wasn't drunk. His mouth was full of foamy blood and it looked to Jago as if he wouldn't keep breathing for much longer.

"Mrs. Tyle!" shouted Jago, looking up toward the open doorway. "Mrs. Tyle!"

After what seemed like several minutes Mrs. Tyle finally appeared at the top of the steps.

"I'm busy! What d'you want?"

"You've got to get him indoors—he needs water, and a doctor!"

Mrs. Tyle, however, wasn't having any of it.

"Him? He's nothing but a stinking old soak! He's puked in the parlor just as I'm ready for visitors. How can folk commune with the spirit world when there's bodies half-dead out the back? Gawdstruth . . ." She turned and disappeared back inside, slamming the door shut behind her.

"Don't leave me!" whispered Callow hoarsely. Jago stared at the old man. Mrs. Tyle's appearance had induced a coughing fit and now flecks of bloody spittle dribbled down his chin and into his beard. Jago didn't know what to do. He couldn't think straight. He knew he ought to grab his things and run because life with his uncle had been a living nightmare and he hated him utterly and completely. Nothing tied him to Callow, who would have left him for dead without a second thought if ever the occasion had arisen. Yet what could the old man do to him now? He couldn't even lift his head off the ground.

Jago went over to a corner of the yard behind the privy, where the shade was at its deepest. The stench from the drain made him gag, but at least it was hidden from the street. No one entering the yard would notice a body lying there.

"C'mon, you stupid old bugger. I've got to shift you."

Callow made no sound as Jago got an arm under each shoulder and dragged him jerkily across the cobbles, but when he was laid out in the shadow of the old yard wall he groaned, pulling his lips back over his gums like a cornered dog.

"You'll be better off here. Mrs. Tyle will fetch help."

Callow's eyes flickered sideways.

"You can't go. . . . You can't leave me. She won't come near me. . . ."

The old man's arthritic fingers caught hold of Jago's shirtsleeve and twisted it. Jago was startled by the strength of his grip. Hadn't he just escaped from Callow's clutches? He ought to run before he was sucked in again—before it was too late. He pulled his arm free and stood up, ready to go. Just then, however, someone else came into the yard.

"This is the place. D'you think she's started?" Jago stepped back into the shadows. The speaker was a pinched-looking young woman in a faded muslin dress. She was leaning on the arm of an older woman—her mother perhaps.

"No, not yet," said her companion. "She likes a full house for a séance. Says it makes the spirits more talkative. Last time the table moved and her chair went all shaky. . . . Gives me the shivers just thinking about it!"

The pair climbed the steps to the door and, after knocking awhile, were eventually admitted. Mrs. Tyle poked her head out and glared at the patch of shadow where Callow lay before banging the door shut once more.

"How many is she expecting?" muttered Jago. He didn't want to bump into any more of Mrs. Tyle's clients as he made a run for it. Perhaps he ought to wait a minute or two. Callow, however, was struggling to say something.

"She's got the gift, boy." He coughed painfully and his lips glistened with phlegm. "Go and ask her something for me."

Callow had always been drawn to the self-proclaimed psychics and mediums they met out on the road. They were frauds, the lot of them as far as Jago was concerned, but Callow wouldn't listen when Jago told him about the hidden wires and secret levers that caused "Madame Poffery" to float above the table and "Signor Cascado" to hear the voices of the recently dead, echoing back from another more mystical dimension. Despite his own career as a con man, Callow believed in the stories about apparitions and ectoplasm perhaps because he needed to believe in something.

"Jago boy, get her to ask the spirits if I'm goin' to die."

Die? Jago looked down at the old man. It hadn't occurred to him that Callow might actually die. Yet when he breathed, a strange bubbling sound came from his chest and his lips were tinged with blue. Most telling of all, though, was the fear in his half-closed eyes. Callow knew that he might not make it through the day.

"It's just tricks, Callow. Tricks as bad as yours. The floating ghosts are lantern slides. Haven't you seen her push the table to make it move? The secret voices probably come from her own children shouting out messages in the room next door."

Callow closed his swollen eyelids. He seemed to be slipping into unconsciousness. Jago, however, felt strangely angry. For years he'd put up with Callow's lies, his cheating, his violence and his stupid fumblings with the conjuror's craft. Most of the time he'd absorbed the blows and the hurt like a dumb animal, waiting for something better, watching his back, quietly refining his own skills in the art of illusion. Now though, he had escaped, for Callow was going to die and he would be free. Yet it wasn't enough. He wanted to shake Callow, to tell him what he knew, to have the old man acknowledge him and finally admit that Jago was cleverer, smarter, better.

"It's all fake!" he shouted in the old man's ear. "You're a fake!"

A dusty jackdaw on top of the wall flapped its black

wings at Jago's outburst, but it didn't fly away. The house, the street were silent. The only noise came from a fat bluebottle fly, buzzing thickly near Callow's oozing wounds. Callow lifted a hand to his head.

"I don't want to die," he whispered, barely audible above the bluebottle's racket.

Jago watched the fly as it landed on Callow's cheek. Was there life after death? Clara had believed in heaven and he'd never needed the likes of Mrs. Tyle to hear her voice, speaking to him inside his head. But what lay in store for gutter types like Callow when they died? The fly would still exist, laying its eggs in anything dead and decaying. Yet that wasn't what Callow wanted to hear. He still hoped for a trick of the light. Jago looked up at the sky.

"I've heard that there are some men of science—like that Mr. Darwin, and Mr. Reade—who reckon we're nothing but a tiddly blink in the grand business of the universe. We're just tiny drops in some giant ocean of life that has existed for millions of years and will go on existing long after we and the rest of humankind have snuffed it."

"Worthless, then," croaked Callow bitterly.

"No, not worthless. By living and by dying we each add a bit of ourselves to a pool of knowledge that moves the universe forward—evolution, I think they call it. We are all joined like a family—made of the same stuff as the plants and animals—even rocks and the stars in the sky."

"So we are all family . . . ," repeated Callow slowly, as though he was trying out a new word. "Now that's a very particular notion."

Jago extracted Clara's letter-block from his blood-encrusted jacket, then leaned back against the wooden shed that housed the privy. The stench filled his nostrils, but he knew it was only a bad smell. Nothing more.

The old man's mouth was twitching oddly. Jago sat up and looked at him closely to check if he was still breathing, but Callow hadn't died yet. He was trying to speak.

"As we're all family, then . . . you won't mind me passing on a few of me secrets, will yer?"

Jago didn't answer. He was sitting with Callow, and that was enough as far as he was concerned. He didn't want to be burdened with the old man's deathbed confessions. Callow, however, was struggling to get his words out.

"When your sister died, I took you in. I'm not blood family though—never have been. I came off a ship and told Clara I was your long-lost uncle—she was dyin' and I didn't want all them books she had to go to waste. I took 'em all and sold 'em and, 'cos I'm not an 'eartless type, I took you too."

"What . . . ?" Jago stared at Callow, trying to take it all in. The old man's face was swimming in front of him, contorted, mocking him it seemed. He stood up, struggling to speak the words that were screaming to get out.

"You filthy, thieving scum! You lied to my sister! You stole her books! They should've come to me! They would have meant so much to me!"

Callow, however, didn't seem to hear.

"Got a bit of money for 'em—not as much as I'd've liked on account of she'd scribbled little ditties to you in most of 'em. Still, I had enough to buy a few props, a few odds and ends. . . . I brung you up, Jago, to follow in me footsteps. I always felt like we was family, and now I want you to sell the cart . . . get me a proper burial. I don't want to rot in no pauper's grave. . . ."

The old man was mumbling now, his tongue thick with effort. Jago didn't hear anymore. He slumped down against the wall and buried his face between his knees. Callow wasn't confessing. He wasn't asking forgiveness for the way he had treated Jago—he actually thought Jago owed him a debt. Even at the point of death, Callow could still act the bully, manipulating Jago's feelings and playing on guilt that had no right to be there. He felt empty suddenly. Not angry, just empty. Perhaps Callow was right—perhaps they had been family. Callow wasn't his uncle, but he was still the person with whom Jago had spent the biggest part of his life. Of course Jago had hated him, but the hate had helped him to survive. Callow couldn't change—he was still a bitter, blind old fool, yet for the first time Jago felt a strange sense of connection with the man who now lay dying in front of him. Callow needed Jago. He actually needed him. It took Jago a moment or two to absorb the shock, but as the thought took hold he felt as though a heavy weight had been lifted away, leaving him with something strange and new. He didn't hate him anymore. Callow had hurt him in every way possible, but what could he do to him now? For the first time in his life, Jago pitied him.

He turned his head, but there was nothing further to be said. Hidden behind a stinking privy and accompanied by the buzzing of a single drowsy fly, Callow had died.

9

The Séance

Jago closed his eyes and leaned his head against the flinty wall. A rat scurried along the far boundary of the yard and from beyond came the haphazard shouts of children playing in the street. The city was still alive, still laboring, struggling, surviving, yet for a few moments Jago simply couldn't comprehend the continuation of everyday sights and sounds. He was separate somehow. His world had changed.

Callow's body lay mangled beside him. The old man was dead; but he hadn't merely died—he had been murdered, and the events that had led to the previous day's attack were clamoring for attention once more. Jago knew he had to run, of course. Armbruster would undoubtedly return to Mrs. Tyle's sooner or later, looking for him. Yet Jago was also beginning to realize that he couldn't simply abandon Callow to the jackdaws and the flies. Perhaps there was a debt to be paid, after all. The old man had wanted a proper burial. An expensive funeral wasn't something Jago could provide, but he could try to secure a little dignity for Callow's body, at least.

Jago straightened out Callow's crumpled arms and legs, placed a piece of sacking over his swollen head and stood up. He would run away anywhere and by any means, but first he would speak to Mrs. Tyle. She wouldn't like it, but

Callow had died on her property and she was going to have to deal with his remains sooner or later.

The house loomed sullenly above Jago as he climbed the steps to the back door. The rickety sash windows were shut as usual, and the sunbaked brickwork was almost too hot to touch. Jago knocked lightly, but there was no sound from inside. He tried the handle. It turned easily enough, although Mrs. Tyle had taken the trouble to secure the door with a chain and it opened by a mere half inch.

With the speed of an expert housebreaker Jago thrust his skinny hand through the gap and twisted his fingers around, feeling for the little brass mounting. A quick flick and the chain was free. He pushed the door open and stepped into the gloom of the hallway, half-expecting to be greeted by Mrs. Tyle's derisive swearing, but still he heard nothing. The house was completely silent. No shouting, no wheezing or coughing, no scuttling of mice. Jago walked along the passage toward the front room where Callow had been beaten up. The place seemed more cluttered than usual and Jago saw the old man's battered bag of knives in a shadowy corner. Mrs. Tyle had clearly wasted no time in plundering the contents of Callow's cart for her own nefarious needs.

The house wasn't empty, however. As Jago stood still, listening, wondering whether to call out, he heard the sharp sound of scraping wood, like a chair or a table being pushed along the bare floor. The sound came from behind the closed parlor door.

Jago moved closer and put his ear to the door. He was

immediately rewarded with a faint but theatrical wail, followed by several short, startled gasps.

Of course. Mrs. Tyle was holding a séance.

Jago put his hand on the grimy doorknob and turned it carefully, pushing the door open by the merest fraction. Through the crack he could see that the window had been covered with a dirty sheet, but a candle flickering on a shelf cast a fickle glimmer over the proceedings. Jago could just make out several figures sitting around a small hexagonal table. Some sort of tattered old screen stood in one corner. As Jago's eyes adjusted to the poor light he realized that Mrs. Tyle sat facing the door, but her eyes were closed and her head was bowed so he assumed that his intrusion had gone unnoticed. The room was as hot as an oven and stank of something stale and sharp like vinegar, or vomit.

The two women greeted by Mrs. Tyle in the yard earlier sat on either side of her, perspiring freely, and a fourth woman had now joined them though Jago could not see her face. They were all holding hands across the heavily fringed chenille cloth that covered the table. Very neat too, to Jago's mind. No one would be able to see what tricks the old woman was pulling in the gloom underneath. What a bunch of fools. . . .

However, just as Jago was about to step into the room to interrupt her little game, he heard a voice he recognized.

"Mrs. Tyle, can you help me communicate with a . . . a dead person? Can you contact Mr. John Piggott of Flint-lock Grange, recently deceased?"

Jago stepped back from the door, no longer wanting to

make himself known. The woman making the request was Anna. How on earth had she come to know about Mrs. Tyle? What did she think she was doing? He took a deep breath and peered into the room once more.

Mrs. Tyle hadn't replied to Anna's request. She had, nevertheless, begun to sway, rocking her body back and forth as though moved by some invisible force. Then she started to moan. She didn't vary the pitch; the sound she made was a low, almost mechanical hum that droned around the airless room, monotonous and interminable.

"What is she doing?" Jago could just about hear Anna whispering to the older woman on her left.

"Ssh! She'll let us know when she's good an' ready!"

Yet after a few minutes even the older woman seemed to be struggling with her impatience, squirming in her seat and dipping her head to wipe the sweat from her face with her shoulder. Jago was beginning to wonder when Mrs. Tyle was going to notice her audience's frustration when all of a sudden she stopped moaning, threw back her head, opened her eyes and began to speak. The voice that came from her mouth was not, however, her own, but that of a frail, well-to-do old man.

"What do you want, child?"

Jago heard Anna's sharp intake of breath. He couldn't see her face, but her voice was trembling when she answered.

"Mr. Piggott, sir? Is it really you? I . . . I want to know what happened to your money. What did you intend for Mr. Robert?"

The room was silent, for a moment. Mrs. Tyle was staring straight ahead, straight toward the door, though

Jago was sure she couldn't see him lurking behind it in the dark. Then she opened her mouth and the old man's voice echoed around the room once more.

"Beware the son! Beware the son!"

"No!" cried Anna, letting go of the others' hands and scraping back her chair. "Not Robert! I can't believe it!"

But Mrs. Tyle hadn't finished.

"And his thieving accomplice, the one called... Stonecipher!"

At this Jago let out a loud snort of derision. He'd heard enough and Mrs. Tyle obviously knew he was hiding there—the game was up. He swung open the door and marched across to the little table, pulling off the chenille cloth with one swift flick of his wrist.

"It's a hoax!" he shouted, pointing out the holes cut into the tabletop so that Mrs. Tyle could poke her toes up beneath the cloth to make glasses wobble and plates spin. "Don't you know that there's a man hidden over there in the corner, throwing his voice to make it sound as though it's coming from Mrs. Tyle!"

Anna was staring, her eyes wide with disbelief.

"But Mr. Piggott *spoke* to me."

"Well let's take a look then, shall we?" Jago strode over to the shabby wooden screen and pulled it aside. The screen clattered noisily to the floor and Mrs. Tyle swore long and loud, for Jago was right, there was someone concealed behind it, sitting on a straight-backed chair. It wasn't a man, though. It was Miss Catherine Piggott. Had the voice of old Mr. Piggott come from her?

Suddenly everyone was shouting.

"How dare you come in 'ere, accusing me of all sorts,

you dirty little picklock!" screamed Mrs. Tyle, jumping up and grabbing Jago by his hair so that he yelped with pain and shock.

"I only came to tell you that Callow's body is lying outside, murdered, and that you'll have to tell the police—get off me, you old witch!" Jago wriggled free, leaving a handful of hair behind in Mrs. Tyle's clenched fist.

"I want my money back!" demanded the older woman from Middle Brook Street.

"What's she doing there? Has she been conning us?" Her daughter stared quite openly at Miss Piggott's fine clothes.

"I think we've heard enough," said Miss Piggott, standing up and smoothing out her black silk skirts. "Anna, where is my reticule?" Anna, nervous and shaking, handed her a little velvet bag, and Miss Piggott took out some coins, which she dropped into the palms of the two dissatisfied women. "That should be ample remuneration. Now please leave us."

The women stared up at her for a moment before looking at the money, then scuttled out of the room without another word. Miss Piggott had been more than generous. Jago, meanwhile, was watching her with undisguised suspicion. He knew all about Mrs. Tyle's little game, and even just about accepted Anna's need to consult her in her desperation to find out the truth about Mr. Piggott's fortune. But what was Catherine Piggott doing at a dingy little lodging house, hiding behind screens and such like? She couldn't possibly believe in all this claptrap.

"You wonder why I am here," said Miss Piggott, as

though reading Jago's mind. "Poor Anna has been so disturbed by recent events that she insisted on consulting a medium to try to establish the truth about my father's intentions. I have always considered that there is little wisdom to be gained from such performances, but I gave her permission to come here in the hope that her mind would be calmed. I confess too that I felt a little curious as to what actually takes place at a séance, and so arranged with Mrs. Tyle to sit behind a screen in order that I might observe without being observed." Miss Piggott glanced briefly at Mrs. Tyle, but the old shyster was for once holding her tongue, bending down to pick up the fallen cloth and straighten the table.

"However, if—as you say—your Mr. Callow has died, then this is serious indeed and the police must be informed immediately."

At mention of the police, Mrs. Tyle opened her mouth to protest but then seemed to reconsider, clamping her lips together as though to prevent any stray mischief from escaping.

"He was murdered," repeated Jago, quieter now.

"As you say," murmured Miss Piggott. Anna sat down suddenly, pale and apparently close to fainting, but her mistress was busy looking for something in her little velvet bag.

"You have had the most dreadful shock, Jago. I generally carry a few smelling salts with me when I am visiting the poor and elderly of the parish. I add a few crushed herbs—just some sage and a little feverfew—and while I would not wish to flatter myself, I am told that the result is most invigorating." Miss Piggott opened her palm and revealed a small bottle containing a few powdery green crystals which she held out to Jago. "Please, inhale a little to steady your nerves. Then we can decide how best to proceed."

Jago closed his eyes for a moment. Miss Piggott was right. His head was spinning. He was exhausted and thoughts tumbled around inside his head, fleeing from sense or logic like the knots in a conjuror's handkerchief. For the first time in years he simply wanted someone else to tell him what to do. His fingers were still curled around the letter-block that he had retrieved from his blood-stained jacket outside and he tightened his fist, silently willing Clara to help him. But the magic was gone, for he couldn't hear his sister's voice. Clara had gone.

Jago took the smelling salts and held them up to his nose, sniffing deeply. The invading fumes smelled sweeter than he had expected and he held the bottle up to the candlelight. The writing on the little yellow label was elegant and even: CATHERINE PIGGOTT'S RESTORATIVE SALTS, FLINTLOCK GRANGE, SAINT CROSS. Strange—something seemed oddly familiar. Jago stared at the label again. It was unusual for *Saint* to be spelled out in full—the word was commonly abbreviated to *St.* Jago had seen *Saint Cross* somewhere before, but where? Then it hit him.

"You!" he shouted, closing his fist around the bottle and taking a step toward Miss Piggott. "You wrote the note in the watch! You and Armbruster together!" The truth was staring him in the face. Miss Piggott seemed taken aback by his outburst and Anna's eyes were wide with fear as Jago staggered forward, but for some reason his eyes wouldn't focus properly.

"Murderer!" he shouted, except that no words came from his mouth. He shook his head, trying to get rid of the strange, creeping numbness that seemed to be affecting his limbs. He had to get out of the house, run away as he'd meant to do all along, yet he felt so giddy and unsteady on his feet. He lunged toward the door and crashed his way past Callow's paraphernalia down the hall. The back door was still open as he had left it, and the bright afternoon sun almost blinded him after the gloom of Mrs. Tyle's parlor. He stumbled down the steps, vision blurred, legs ready to give way. There were shouts behind him—Jago thought he heard a man's voice and heavy, big-booted footsteps before Mrs. Tyle joined in, yelling and swearing.

"There 'e goes, the little magpie! Where's my money? You can't go down there till you've paid for the privilege!"

The yard gate was shut. Jago leaned against it, pushing with what little strength he had left, but he couldn't get it open. His arms felt like rubber and his legs were about to buckle beneath him.

"Poison!" he wanted to shout. "Murder!" But then he felt a blow to the back of his head that deadened his brain and stopped his cry like a mouthful of dry sawdust left behind from the fair.

10

Escape

There was thunder. From all around came a low, ominous rumbling that didn't stop. It caught him up and shook him, pounding against his skull, bruising his brain. Jago dreamed he was harnessed once more to Callow's old cart, pulling the deadweight over flint-strewn ground, straining and heaving till his muscles screamed, but he couldn't stop, for the track wound on and on through the cold starless night, never ending, never easing.

Everything hurt. Jago opened his eyes, but still the world was black. His head was jammed between his knees and his elbows pressed against something hard and unforgiving on either side, as though he were back inside Callow's trunk performing The Miracle of One Thousand Cuts. This trunk, however, was moving.

Jago shifted his feet to brace himself better and tried to focus on what had happened to him. The air he sucked into his lungs felt cool, as though it was nighttime. His body was knocking painfully from side to side, and there were sounds too, of pounding hooves and rushing wind, of jangling harnesses and crunching wheels. He was squashed inside a trunk on a horse-drawn coach or cart, and the horses were galloping hard.

Jago pushed his shoulders up against the roof of the trunk, but the lid, of course, was locked. This trunk had no secret mechanism or hidden door; he was trapped and panic began to make its presence felt in his knotted muscles and thumping heart. He knew he had to calm down so that his brain and not his body could take control and get him out. A wiry escapologist he had met at a fair in Salisbury had told him how her skill was all in her breathing—steady, shallow breaths, in through the mouth and out through the nose. Subdue the fear—that was it. Breathe in, breathe out. . . .

But Jago's breath was knocked right out of him as he was suddenly shunted with skull-smacking force against the back of the trunk. The horses must have dragged the wheels across a particularly large pothole and from somewhere in front of him a man's voice shouted and cursed above the tortured sounds of scraping metal and fractured wood. Yet despite much frenzied whinnying the carriage did not stop. The sharp crack of a whip cut through the thunderous pounding of hooves and it was clear that the driver was pushing the horses harder than ever.

Jago was used to bruises, but the fierce jolting now seemed to be causing something sharp to stab him in the thigh. The pain made his eyes water. Once again he was reliving the nightmare of Callow's trunk and the knives that came a little too close for comfort. Nevertheless, he found that if he squeezed his right elbow toward his rib cage, he could just about twist his hand to touch the cold shaft of a rusty nail that had worked its way loose, so that it now poked out of the wooden side panel by about half an inch.

Loose nails, false panels. These were things that Jago

understood. These were the tools of his trade, the instruments of illusion.

He had little room in which to maneuver, of course. His right hand was badly positioned against his side, and he couldn't grasp the end of the nail with sufficient freedom to pull it out. He did have a lever, however. Pinching the fraying cloth of his trouser pocket between thumb and forefinger, he felt for the small, hard lump that lay hidden inside. Clara's letter-block. If he could just work it a little farther up his leg, it would reach the pocket opening and drop into his waiting palm. There he had it. With stiff fingers he jammed the letter-block up behind the jutting nail, and pulled. The nail was forced out of the wood just as Jago's fingers slipped and lost their grip.

Breathe in, breathe out. His head ached blindingly and he was still half-dazed from the anesthetizing effects of Catherine Piggott's "salts," yet Jago knew that he had to get out of the trunk. Was he supposed to be dead? Why was he being moved? In the space of a few hours, his world had been ripped apart. His brain screamed at him to believe nothing and trust no one. Callow, Anna, Catherine Piggott, nobody was as they seemed. Even Clara had betrayed him, for Jago could no longer hear her voice.

His kidnapper had not bothered to bind his arms and legs, relying instead on a padlock and chain to secure the ancient trunk. It seemed that no one had been expecting Jago to wake up. He shifted again, this time wedging his left foot firmly into a corner, and took a deep breath. On his own silent count of three he tensed his muscles, pushing outward, forcing his right shoulder up against the side of the trunk. The loose nail had been enough. The wooden panel simply fell away, leaving Jago exposed to the overwhelming rush of cold air that whipped past his face and made him gasp with shock. It took a moment to orient himself, but as soon as he could move his stiffened limbs he crouched low and hung on grimly to the ropes that secured the trunk. For he was on the open roof of a carriage that was hurtling through the night at heart-stopping speed.

Jago soon abandoned any thought of jumping off. The carriage was moving too fast for anyone to survive such a fall. The driver was hunched over the reins, bending into the wind. Jago couldn't see his face but he knew from the heavy set of his shoulders that the man had to be Armbruster. There was only one way to get off without being noticed. Jago guessed that the horses would have to slow down soon because no animal could sustain such a headlong, reckless pace for long. His best hope was to hold on until the horses tired, then leap off before the carriage came to a complete stop.

A pale new moon had risen, its eerie luminescence revealing the chalky highway ahead. Jago glimpsed trees, hedges and a dim blanket of fields that folded into the night. The carriage climbed a steep hill and the horses snorted and lowered their heads with the effort, but all too soon they were over the brow and beginning their descent, hurtling down the gradient like wild-eyed run-aways. However, just as Jago was beginning to doubt whether he would be able to hold on for much longer, Armbruster pulled sharply on the reins and the horses slackened their pace. He saw lights ahead, and a few scattered cottages. The carriage was stopping.

Jago inched his way to the edge of the carriage roof, looking for a soft grassy spot to break his fall. He had chosen his spot and was just about to jump when, from out of the darkness, someone shouted.

"Armbruster!"

Jago held back. It was Catherine Piggott's voice, coming from the carriage beneath him. It hadn't occurred to him that there might be passengers inside. What if she saw him jump?

"Armbruster!" She sounded angry. "Why are we stopping?"

"The horses want water." Armbruster spoke curtly, pulling the horses off the road and drawing up in front of a long, low-thatched building as he did so. A lantern had been lit on either side of the heavy oak front door, and Jago could just make out the name on a peeling sign above the lintel: THE OTTERBOURNE ARMS. They had stopped at a coaching inn on the road to Southampton.

A boy in short breeches appeared and caught hold of the horses' bridles while Armbruster leaped down from his seat and opened the carriage door.

"I need to have a word around the back. Stay here."

"Don't speak to me like that." Jago crouched low as Catherine Piggott emerged from the carriage, lifting her skirts and treading warily across the dirty cobblestones. "I shall take some refreshment while you deal with matters out here. Come, Anna."

Jago peered down from behind the trunk to see Anna push open the door to the inn and then step back to allow her mistress to enter first. Anna wore a hooded cape and her eyes were lowered, but in the lanterns' pool of greenish light Jago could tell that one cheekbone was a vivid red as though she had been slapped across her face.

Armbruster followed Anna into the inn. The boy holding the bridles began to lead the horses, still harnessed to the carriage, around the side of the building and into a straw-strewn stable yard. The animals stopped in front of a water trough and immediately bent their heads to drink. They were tired and thirsty and the boy didn't stand around to keep an eye on them but strolled off and disappeared into the shadows. The yard fell silent, apart from the occasional snorting of the horses as they drank their fill.

This was the moment Jago had been waiting for. No one was watching. He swung his body over the side of the carriage and dropped quickly to the ground. Beyond the gates of the yard, darkness beckoned. Jago wasn't going to make any more mistakes, however. Armbruster was bound to be lurking about somewhere so scrambling over the back wall and running across the fields would, he guessed, offer his best chance of escape.

As he moved around the side of the carriage he glanced through an open window. The seats were comfortably upholstered and the doors were lined with velvet. On the floor lay a lady's escritoire—a folding writing case with little drawers for pens and paper. Jago looked away and was about to run toward the wall when it occurred to him that the escritoire might be worth something. He had no money. Catherine Piggott had kidnapped him, tried to have him killed. Taking something from her in order to help himself could hardly be called theft.

Jago opened the door and leaned forward to grab the

escritoire, ready to run. Something, however, made him pause. He looked down at the case he was holding, his fingers tracing the delicate pattern of leaves that had been tooled into the soft leather. He was better than the likes of Armbruster and Catherine Piggott. He shivered suddenly and replaced the escritoire. He wasn't going to steal from them. He wasn't going to allow himself to be tainted by their crimes. He was free.

"So you are alive, then?" The voice behind him spoke clearly, ringing out and cutting through the silence of the shadowy stable yard. Jago spun round, but he could see no one.

"You won't get far. They won't let you get far."

"Who are you? Show yourself!" whispered Jago. The voice had him trapped against the carriage. He couldn't run, because he couldn't see where the danger lay. The voice was familiar though. A woman's voice, but not as deep as Catherine Piggott's. This woman sounded empty and hollow. Dead, even.

"You know who I am," said the voice. Jago was silent, though his heart was thumping and his breath came in shallow gasps. "You told me to stay out of his way, but what about *her*?" There was a footstep on the cobbles, a soft rustle of skirts.

"Clara . . . ," whispered Jago. Could it be his sister? He shut his eyes, trying to erase the confusion that clouded his senses. What was she talking about? What had he told her? He didn't understand, but his confusion was over before it had time to take hold, for it wasn't a ghost that stepped out of the shadows and into the deathly sheen of a pale new moon: it was Anna.

"Take what you can and run, Jago, but it won't do you any good." Anna spoke loudly as though she no longer cared who heard her, her voice brittle with despair and bitterness. Her hood had fallen across her shoulders. Her face was bruised, but worse than that, she looked broken. She was flesh and blood and nerves and bones all right.

"What has happened to you? What have they done to you?"

"It doesn't matter. But you ran off and left me with that woman. I didn't know . . ." Anna's voice faltered and she lowered her eyes.

Jago stepped forward.

"You didn't tell me everything, Anna. You didn't tell me the truth about Catherine Piggott and Armbruster; you must have known what was going on!"

"Don't come near me! I didn't know. I trusted her just like you made me trust you. But now I know the truth, and if you want to know it too, then take the writing case— take it and you'll find out. It won't do any good. . . ."

"What do you mean?" pressed Jago, but suddenly another voice cut into the night.

"Anna! Where is my shawl?" Catherine Piggott was coming.

"Quick! Come with me!" He held out his hand for Anna to take, but she shook her head.

"Not this time, Jago. You'll be better off without me."

She turned abruptly and stepped back into the shadows.

Jago stared after her, uncomprehending. He knew nothing about the Piggotts' money or South America or the ways of lovers. But Callow had been murdered and

Anna was hurt and, somehow, it seemed to be because of him.

"I'll find your Mr. Robert!" he whispered. "I'll tell him what they've done!" Yet Anna was gone. He had no idea whether she had heard him. It felt like a promise, nevertheless.

Somewhere a door slammed and Jago heard the sound of running footsteps. Then Armbruster's voice bellowed from beyond the stable wall.

"They're bringing around fresh horses—we'll be on the road again directly!"

In seconds the yard would be awash with lanterns as new horses were brought out and harnessed up. Jago didn't have a moment to lose. He grabbed the writing case and ran, feet flying across the straw-strewn cobbles, up and over the back wall, dropping down to the field on the other side and vanishing into the silky darkness like a knife up a sleeve.

Part Two

Nerves and Bones

11

Southampton Docks

Jago stood on the steps of the Southampton offices of the Royal Mail Steam Packet Company and peered out across the docks. A damp white mist had rolled up from the sea overnight, veiling the waterfront and transforming the tangle of waterside chimneys and tall mainmasts into a softer, more mysterious landscape. Yet the docks were out there all right. A ship's horn bellowed deafeningly through the bleary air. The din of straining winches, clanking chains and the shouts of the dockyard workers as they loaded coal had been competing with its ear-splitting blasts since half past five that morning.

The door behind Jago opened suddenly and a woman appeared. She wore an elegant fawn-colored day dress that rustled expensively as she walked down the steps, and her face was hidden beneath a fashionably tilted hat. Jago turned away sharply. He pulled his cap down low and studied the steamer itinerary that had been posted in a window above the railing. Well-dressed women were making him jumpy.

Jago had been hanging around the many offices of the different steamship companies since daybreak. He'd been kicked out of a few of their doorways and frowned upon in others, but generally he'd managed to glean a few snippets of information from a passing clerk or messenger boy.

He had learned, for instance, that there were a number

of steamers leaving port that week, shipping emigrants to Montreal, engineers to Cape Town and whiskey and mail to the colonists in the West Indies. None of this was of any use, however, and it wasn't until he reached the smart and somber offices of the Royal Mail Steam Packet Company that he found what he was looking for. That very morning, at eleven o'clock sharp, the RMS *Colorado* was due to sail for Rio de Janeiro. Jago wouldn't be allowed to see the passenger list, but he didn't need to. Mr. Robert Piggott was sure to be on board.

Jago crossed Canute Road, narrowly missing a horse cab that loomed up out of the mist, and began to walk in the direction of the West Dock Gate. His insides ached hollowly—a nagging reminder that he had eaten nothing since the eggs and milk he'd wolfed down at Flintlock Grange the previous day. He had walked all night on an empty stomach, but today's breakfast would just have to wait a little while longer. He had long since tossed the writing case into a hedge, but the papers it had contained were now tucked safely inside his shirt.

The sun was starting to burn through the morning mist, dissolving it into a filmy haze. Jago breathed in the smells of salt, rotting seaweed and engine oil, and raised his face to catch the day's first warmth. Despite his preoccupied state he couldn't help but notice that the dockside road was uncommonly busy. Cabs and carts bustled up and down in the usual way, but the pavement was becoming crowded with people—women, mainly, dressed in their holiday clothes and calling out as they tried to rein in excitable children with shining faces and scrubbed knees. Yet it wasn't until Jago rounded a bend and saw the dock gate decked out in Union Jack bunting that he remembered the words of a clerk from earlier that morning:

"There's a troop ship coming in from Ashanti—tickets to the quayside for immediate family only."

He walked up behind a plainly dressed mother and her two patched-up children, hoping that he would look like one of the family, but the ticket inspector standing beside the tall iron gates wasn't so easily fooled.

"Hey lad, where's your ticket?"

"Ticket?" Jago tried to sound nonchalant. "Oh yes, my ma's got it. She's already gone through." The inspector, however, frowned and stuck out his arm.

"I don't think so, chum. Go on—get lost!"

Jago was going to have to do things his own way, as usual, but there wasn't much time. He had to speak to Robert Piggott. He had to let him know that Anna was in danger and warn him that his own sister, Catherine, wanted him dead.

As Jago walked further along the road toward the imposing bulk of the South Western Hotel he heard the screeching, grinding sound of a line of goods wagons being shunted along the railway tracks that crisscrossed the docks. The tracks bisected Canute Road itself, shifting cargo between the railway terminus and the quayside. It was always worth trying the back door. If he could climb on a wagon as it crossed the road, he would be transported unseen into the very heart of the docks. This plan was his only hope now, as it was already half past nine and the *Colorado* would surely be hauling up its gangplanks within the hour.

Jago was in luck. As he approached the tracks a line of

wagons was just beginning to jolt its way over the crossing in the road. Pedestrians and horse-drawn vehicles
were already building up on either side as they waited for
the clanking great obstacle to their morning's business
to pass.

"Get out of the bloody way!" shouted one cabdriver,
impatiently stamping on his footplate. Then suddenly a
ship's horn blasted across the docks, and in the three-
second space where ears were covered and protesting
eyes turned toward the waterfront, Jago clambered into a
coal-filled car and was gone.

The old pier on the south side of the outer dock was
teeming with people. A raised platform had been set up
for the official reception committee to welcome home the
troops from West Africa. There were seats for the officers' wives and a good deal of standing room had been
cordoned off for ordinary soldiers' families. Flags and
ribbons of red, white and blue were flapping in the sunshine, and a loud cheer went up as the gangplanks were
lowered and the men began to disembark from the three-
hundred-foot-long steamship.

"Three cheers for our brave boys!" The cry went up and
the crowd responded enthusiastically. "Hip hip hooray!"

From somewhere farther along the pier, a brass band
began to play "God Save the Queen," but by now soldiers
were being greeted and hugged and the orderly welcome
descended into a more chaotic celebration. Hip flasks
were produced and laughing children were swung,
shrieking onto their daddies' shoulders.

The RMS *Colorado* was berthed alongside the newly

arrived troopship. It was an iron screw-propeller steamer, with two masts and a single black funnel rising out of its long, sleek hull. Jago, safely hidden among the soldier-revelers, kept his eyes on the smaller, more businesslike crowd gathered around its central gangplank. For the first time it occurred to him that Robert Piggott might already have embarked. Jago had only seen Piggott twice before—once in darkness by the cathedral and a second time in his cloth cap disguise at Flintlock Grange—but he continued to scrutinize every new arrival. He didn't know what else to do. Besides, Piggott's wasn't the only face that he was looking out for.

It was ten o'clock. From somewhere up above, a whistle blew. Several young men carrying calfskin traveling bags climbed up toward the deck. Prospectors, speculators—keen to find their fortunes overseas, at any rate. Jago wondered how long it would take them. Three weeks sailing to Rio; three years maybe before they returned home fat and happy or ruined and hard-boiled.

There was a sudden flurry of activity at the bottom of the gangplank as a porter wheeling a large trunk pushed through the throng.

"Do be careful! Please don't jolt it like that!" A small woman under a hat piled high with feathers and ribbons was plucking at the porter's sleeve as he tried to steer a path through the crowd. The porter looked hot, and disgruntled too if frowning was anything to go by.

"I'm doing me best, missus! What've you got in there? Runnin' off with the family silver?"

"I beg your pardon—how dare you!" The woman stopped in front of her trunk so that the porter could push it no further. "Maud! Cecily! Cover your ears! I will not be insulted like that! Such insolence!" Two girls appeared from behind the porter, blushing underneath their bonnets. Jago wished heartily that they would all just move on out of the way. They were obscuring his view of the gangplank. The porter, however, had other ideas.

"Right! I've had enough! Here's your sodding trunk, you silly twit!" He pushed the trunk forward so that it tipped off his trolley with a resounding crash. "You can haul it up there yerself, and never mind the shilling!"

"Oh! Oh goodness!" The woman looked as though she was about to crumple up into a heap as the porter disappeared to find himself a more amenable customer. She closed her eyes and clutched her head, swaying a little too theatrically to Jago's mind. Her daughters tried to bring her around, supporting her arms and fanning her face. Clearly they were going to have their work cut out getting *her* up the gangplank, let alone the trunk. Their predicament, however, gave him an idea. He'd have a much better view of the crowd from up on the deck of the mail ship.

"Madam, madam, please let me be of assistance!" Jago stepped forward, grasped a handle of the large leather trunk and began to pull with both hands. The trunk was impossibly heavy—Jago could barely shift it an inch on his own but with two young ladies applauding his gesture he knew it wouldn't be long before some gentleman or other would feel obliged to follow suit. Sure enough, a man with a broad, weathered face in a blue coat with brass buttons was soon pushing the trunk from behind.

"Good day, madam! Chief Officer Morgan at your

service! This really ought to have been forwarded earlier. . . ."

"Oh thank you! Just be careful with it, please—don't drop it!"

With considerable effort and some cheery heave-hoing, the trunk was finally installed under a broad canvas awning on the open upper deck of the ship. While the older daughter thanked Mr. Morgan for his help and went off in search of a deck chair for her mother, the younger daughter turned to Jago.

"That was kind of you! Have you come to entertain us on the crossing? Please say yes!"

Jago frowned at her. She couldn't have been more than eleven. Something about her was familiar, but what was she talking about?

The girl pushed back her bonnet a little and smiled up at him with bright, inquisitive eyes. Then he remembered. She and her sister were the girls who had paid for his dinner in the Black Swan two nights ago. Before he could reply, however, he felt the weight of a firm hand on his shoulder.

"Run along now, lad. We'll not be pretending you're here for the ride, will we?" The captain was standing behind him, come down from the wheelhouse to see what all the fuss was about.

"No, sir," muttered Jago, turning and stepping toward the top of the gangplank. He stared down at the swirling mass of heads and hats, the stacks of crates and piles of luggage, the dispersing soldiers and last-minute passengers, all weaving their chaotic dance on the dockside below him. He hadn't found Mr. Robert. There was nothing else he could do but descend and rejoin the noisy throng.

Yet sometimes change comes faster than the click of a coin-clipper's fingers. As Jago took hold of the rope hand rail, two things happened that altered everything. First he heard a shriek from directly behind him and a thud as something or someone fell onto the varnished wooden deck. Before he could turn his head, however, his eye caught a fleeting glimpse of a figure he recognized in the crowd below before it disappeared behind a trolley piled high with luggage. Armbruster.

For a single moment, a mere half-second, the world stopped moving. The scene in front of Jago became clouded and indistinct. The shouts around him softened to distant murmurs. His senses disconnected themselves from his brain until a single question could penetrate his panic and reality returned in all its sharp focus. Jago stood in full view of everyone on the dockside. Had Armbruster seen him?

He didn't wait to find out. Turning back toward the deck he took in the scene in an instant. The woman with the trunk had fainted in a tangle of lavender tulle. Her two daughters were bending over her, lifting her head while the captain knelt down to feel her pulse. Other passengers and crew were hurrying to see what had happened. A narrow door stood open in front of Jago. It wasn't much of a choice. He didn't pause to wonder what the gloom beyond might hold, but stepped swiftly into its enveloping shadow.

The steamer was preparing to leave. Embarkation horns were sounding, an officer was shouting orders and the crew were hurrying to their stations. The narrow passage at the bottom of the stairs was full of passengers jostling and complaining as they searched for their cabins. No one noticed a ragged boy squeeze past. With instincts sharpened by years of seeking out warm, dry, safe places to hide, Jago made his way like an ocean-bound rat down into the dark iron bowels of the ship.

12
Cecily

Jago hid in an empty locker between the fore hatch and a coalhole for two whole days. The locker was narrow and barely deep enough for him to stretch out his legs, but he was used to confined spaces. The cramp in his thighs and the ache in his shoulders were the least of his troubles. The *Colorado* was a steamship, fueled by coal, powered by vast boilers and driven by an engine room the size of a house. Jago curled up in the oily darkness with his hands over his ears, but he couldn't block out the thunder of crashing pistons that shook along the metal walls and shuddered through his head. Neither could he do anything about his thirst. His tongue swelled in his mouth as his body dehydrated, and though his stomach was too empty to bring up anything more than bile, he was made hideously sick by the rolling, plunging motion of the ship as it steamed across the Bay of Biscay.

Jago dozed fitfully, his dreams punctuated with the shouts and curses of the stokers in the coalhole that mingled disturbingly with other voices in his head.

"You lazy idlebones! Get out of there! Fancied a bit of a jaunt, did you? Well don't be expecting any pennies from me, you little waster, and don't try scamming old Callow again!"

His wakeful moments were no better. What in God's name had he gone and done? He didn't even know if Mr.

Robert was on board. The papers he'd taken were still inside his shirt, but he couldn't examine them in the darkness. By the end of the second day, he was so weak he could barely lick the drops of condensation that had formed on the metal fittings inside the locker door. He'd had enough of his juddering hellhole. He had to find something to drink. He'd rather be discovered alive than dead, but his head was throbbing fit to burst. . . .

Then, just as Jago had begun to dream that a skeleton lay in the darkness beside him—the skeleton of a stowaway with the letter *J* hammered into its skull—he woke up with a start to a faint ringing sound. It took him a few moments to realize that the noise came from inside his own head. The propeller shaft had stopped turning. The rough shouts, the sharp hiss of escaping steam and the nerve-jangling scrape of shovels in the coalhole had ceased. The buzz in his ears was, it seemed, the unexpected and extraordinary sound of silence.

The ship must have reached port somewhere—Coruña or Vigo perhaps, dropping off the mail and picking up more passengers before heading out across the ocean. Maybe the crew had been given some shore leave. Jago pushed open the door of the locker with his foot and groaned out loud as he struggled to reactivate his numbed limbs. Part of him hoped that a passing stoker would find him and drag him out—at least he'd be given a drink—but he saw no one in the dim tunnel of passageway beyond. As he groped his way forward his circulation returned and his legs gave way in an agony of pins and needles. He slumped to the floor and closed his eyes, too weak to stop the drift toward unconsciousness.

"Hooray! I thought I'd find you down here!" The light, singsong voice made him jump and his head pounded with the jolt and his own confusion. He squinted upward. Someone—a girl, surely—was standing directly in front of him, her pale hair gleaming in the sliver of daylight from the hatch way up above her head.

"You don't look very well—have you been seasick?" She knelt down and peered at Jago. "Everyone else has. Anyway, we've reached Spain now and Mr. Morgan—he's the Chief Officer—says that the worst is over, though I don't see how with the whole of the Atlantic still to come. What's it like being a stowaway?"

As the girl chattered on, not seeming to notice that Jago was now bent double on the floor in his struggle to get up, he recognized her for the second time. She was the girl from the Black Swan, the girl whose mother he had helped with her trunk. How did she know he was here? Had she told anyone else? He winced as he got to his knees and then slowly straightened himself out until he stood in front of her, only a little taller and considerably dirtier.

"Have you got anything to drink?"

"Of course! I thought you might be hungry, too!" The girl opened a clumsily crocheted bag she had been clutching, and offered it to Jago. Inside lay two glass-stoppered bottles of ginger ale, a slice of game pie, several tiny sandwiches and a rather misshapen bun.

"I've been saving things from luncheon. I have to be ever so careful or Maud will catch me. Mama would never notice, but Maud is so nosy she finds out all my secrets. I'm not going to let her find out about you, though. You're all mine."

"I didn't think anyone saw me come down here," spluttered Jago, coughing up half of the ginger ale he'd gulped too quickly. "How'd you find me?"

"Oh I've got eyes like a cat, Mama says. I see all sorts of things I'm not supposed to. Like when Mama pretends to faint so that everyone feels sorry for her and we are allowed to travel in a lovely first-class cabin. She steals cutlery you know. That's what's in our trunk. I shouldn't tell you, but then I know your secret so you may as well know mine. I'm Cecily Conway, by the way."

Jago stared at her. He didn't know what to make of her. Could anyone who chattered this much be trusted not to blab? If any of the crew found him he'd be thrown off the ship at the nearest port, which might not in different circumstances be so bad, but he had made a promise to Anna. He still had to find Mr. Robert. Nevertheless, now that the ginger ale had cleared his head, he knew that he couldn't just go roaming about the ship looking for him. Cecily might be useful. What did he have to lose?

"I need help," he said, looking her straight in the eye, secret to secret.

"That's exactly what I hoped you'd say!" she exclaimed, beaming like a cat that had got the canary. "And you shall help me too! I want you to teach me some of your tricks!"

True to her word, Cecily proved to be extremely useful. By the time the *Colorado* had left the coast of Portugal and was steaming toward Madeira, she had smuggled down two candles and some matches, a heavy stone bedwarmer full of cold tea, half a dozen breakfast rolls and a

109

cushion embroidered with the Royal Mail Steam Packet Company insignia. She was inventive too. She told Jago that she had made friends with the ship's cat, a black-and-white tom called Twisty that prowled about the holds and feasted on rats and mice. Cecily wasn't supposed to descend into the working areas of the ship, but on the few occasions when she had been discovered she explained herself by saying that she was looking for the cat. The Chief Officer in particular was very indulgent, and Cecily reported that he had even invited her down below for a tour of the engine room.

Jago had been quick to ask Cecily whether she had encountered a passenger by the name of Mr. Robert Piggott, but here she was less able to help.

"Most of the passengers are keeping to their cabins. Mama isn't well, but she still gets up for dinner. There's a newfangled fan in the dining room that makes her feel better. Mr. Morgan says that some people don't get over their seasickness until they step back onto dry land."

"What about a Mr. Armbruster?"

Cecily shook her head.

"No, I don't think so. Why do you want to know?" Jago looked away. She tried again. "Who *are* these people?" Still he stayed silent. He had absolutely no intention of sharing any more of his secrets.

"Right." She raised an eyebrow, which made her look more knowing than her years. "Like that, is it?"

Now she had gone too far. Jago didn't want her assuming things he didn't fully understand himself.

"Like *what*? Look, you don't know anything about me!

I'm grateful all right for the food and stuff, but just keep your nose out of my business!" Cecily's brow crinkled into a hurt frown, and he immediately regretted his outburst. She was just a wide-eyed child. All the same, she had an uncanny knack for hitting the nail on the head.

The *Colorado*'s call at Madeira was brief, as there were no more passengers to pick up before the Cape Verde Islands. Jago's seasickness seemed to subside as the ship steamed out into the Atlantic, and with the help of the smuggled provisions he soon regained his strength. Cecily reported that the weather was calm, and getting hotter by the day.

"Some passengers are still suffering, mind you," she commented, unwrapping a sticky, custard-filled pastry from her handkerchief and handing it to Jago. "I often hear crying in the cabin next to ours. Some poor girl is feeling really under the weather. I wanted to knock on the door to see if I could cheer her up, but Maud won't let me. She says I'm always interfering, but I know that if I was poorly, I'd be glad of visitors. Anyway, I want you to teach me that trick you told me about with the saltcellar." She rummaged in her little crocheted bag. "Look—I took it at luncheon!"

As Cecily held up the dainty crystal and silver cruet set it occurred to Jago that she had picked up a few tricks from her mother already.

"You mustn't take things like that," he muttered, remembering with a sudden stab how he had learned to steal by watching Callow.

"Don't tell me you've never stolen anything!" exclaimed

Cecily, quite shocked, it seemed, to discover that he was a stowaway with scruples. Jago sighed.

"Just promise me you'll put it back later." She was already a thief. It made him feel tired.

Now that Jago had candles and matches, he began to examine the bundle of papers he had taken from Catherine Piggott's writing case. The papers had suffered under his shirt. Most were crumpled, a little torn, damp from sweat and smudged, and it took Jago a while to sort them into various piles according to type. First there were a number of handwritten receipts in a foreign language that seemed to relate to amounts of money adding up to several tens of thousands of pounds. Then there were several letters from old Mr. Piggott to a "Senhor Carvalho," written in English and concerning the transfer of funds to a bank account in Rio. This must have been for the purpose of investing in the sewer scheme, and the fact that these letters had since come into Catherine Piggott's possession seemed suspicious enough. However, there were other letters, some from Catherine Piggott to Armbruster and one rather stained envelope with the words *Casa do Paraiso* written in a spidery scrawl across the front. Jago held up his candle to peer more closely at the yellowy blotches beneath the words. It looked as though the darker areas formed a definite shape. The shape of a key. The envelope was empty now, but Jago guessed that it had once held a key, which, over time, had left its imprint on the paper. Was this the key that Anna had taken? She hadn't explained what it was for.

Someone was coming. Jago heard the thud of heavy

footsteps in the passageway outside. He blew out his candle and held his breath. He knew that his hiding place was on the bottom deck near the front of the ship. A corridor ran up toward some storerooms in the bow. Footsteps weren't unusual. However, these ones had come to a stop.

"I think I saw him go down that way!" It was Cecily. Her high, singsong voice was unmistakable.

"All right, poppet, don't fret yourself. We'll find him sooner or later. You get back up to your mama, now." This time the speaker was a man. What was Cecily doing? Was she about to give the game away? It was clear to Jago that her interest in him was merely her way of relieving the tedium of life on board the *Colorado*. Was she about to liven things up a little more?

The locker door was pulled open with a sharp tug. Jago scrunched up his eyes as the light from a swinging oil lamp flooded in, but the face peering down at him was Cecily's and, thankfully, she appeared to be alone.

"Hello! Did you hear us looking for Twisty? Mr. Morgan walked right past!"

Jago didn't know whether to be relieved or angry.

"I thought you were about to tell him where I was!"

"Why would I do that?" She looked hurt. "He's been showing me the engine room, and I wanted him to go away so that I could come and see you. I've sent him off on a wild-goose chase looking for Twisty. The soft old thing is actually up in the dining saloon, fast asleep under the sideboard. I've brought you an orange. I thought you'd be pleased."

Jago had underestimated Cecily. She was playful all right, but he ought to trust her. He relit his candle and shifted farther back into the locker's narrow space to make room for her by way of an apology.

"What's all this?" she asked, pulling her pinafore dress up around her knees and squeezing in beside him. Jago looked down at the papers he had spread out on the narrow stretch of floor between his feet and began to shuffle them back together.

"Just some old letters."

"Oh—love letters?" asked Cecily, her eyes sparkling in the candle's fluttering light.

"No, nothing like that. Just private letters."

"From your family then?"

Once again Cecily had touched a raw nerve. How could he begin to explain about the packet of letters, the evidence they contained about a plot to steal tens of thousands of pounds, and the murderous intentions of the people who had written them? How could he begin to explain about his promise to Anna or that he had no family, that his sister had died and the man he had hated for being his uncle turned out not to have been his own flesh and blood after all? He carried these things deep inside, and much of the pain they inflicted was still too fresh to fully comprehend.

Yet Cecily, he sensed, had been nothing but honest with him. Despite her mother's acting and her own precocious talent as a pilferer, she welcomed the world with open arms and had probably never lied to herself in all her life.

"I had a sister," he began. "Her name was Clara. She taught me to read."

"Oh, reading . . ." Cecily rolled her eyes comically. "I hate it. Mama wants me to read some of Maud's old books while we're on board. They're deadly dull. *The Young Lady's Guide to Modest Deportment. The Misses Hartley Visit Leamington Spa. Langdon's Compleat Silver Hallmarks.* I don't care about being a proper lady or how much a spoon is worth! Maud's much better at all that sort of thing."

"Don't you read stories—novels?"

"Novels? I'm not allowed to read them. Mama says they are corrupting."

"Corrupting!" Jago snorted. "Mr. Dickens doesn't corrupt. He makes you see a bigger world, that's all. He writes about people—about love and pain and truth and lies. . . ."

"Tell me one of his stories, please!"

Jago was silent for a moment. Those tales were embedded in his memory. He carried them everywhere, but they bore the imprint of his sister's voice. How could he begin to speak them to someone else? Yet when Jago opened his mouth to begin, he found that it was his voice, his cadence that gave life to the words that Clara had given him. Could she hear him? Was she somewhere in the shadows behind Jago's shoulder? As Cecily drank in the drama of an orphan called Oliver Twist, he was the teller and Clara, perhaps, was the listener.

13

Cabin Nineteen

"We've seen dolphins!" Cecily was calling to Jago before she had even opened the locker door.

"Quiet!" he hissed, though it wasn't her voice that he feared would give him away—the din from the boiler room provided excellent cover. Cecily was far more likely to be seen than heard, and it seemed to Jago that she was taking risks. Twisty the cat had proved to be female, producing a litter of kittens beneath the sideboard in the dining saloon. Cecily was delighted and she refused to admit that Twisty's new responsibilities left her without a plausible excuse should she be found wandering below the passenger decks.

"It's so hot we had luncheon on deck today—I was the first to spot them in the water! The Cape Verde Islands are off the port bow and we're taking on coal at St. Thomas this afternoon. Oh, that reminds me, I've met your Mr. Piggott."

After eight suffocating days at sea this was good news at last.

"Are you sure it's Piggott?" asked Jago, reaching past her to close the door as she knelt down beside him.

"Mr. Morgan introduced us—Maud was blushing like mad. Mama sat next to him and they talked about Brazil. We had cold cuts for luncheon. I've brought you some ham. Mr. Piggott didn't eat much though—still a bit wobbly, I should think." She wrinkled her nose. "Jago, I don't want to be rude, but did you know that it smells absolutely disgusting in here?"

"Where is his cabin?" asked Jago, ignoring her question and putting the cushion she'd given him over the bucket he'd been using to pee in.

"I don't know, but I'm sure I could find out. Second class forward, first class aft! Did you know that stairs are called companionways? I've been learning ship-talk from Mr. Morgan!"

Jago smiled. He might not actually have been on a ship before, but he had lived on the dockside at Portsmouth for long enough to know the difference between port and starboard. Still, she was enjoying showing off.

"There aren't actually many passengers on board. Mama says twenty-one first class and thirteen second. Apparently there's been another yellow fever scare in Rio, though that didn't put Mama off and I think I know why. She might have been arrested if we stayed in England!"

Jago looked at Cecily. Not yet twelve years old, well fed, well dressed and well on the way to becoming a proper young lady. Yet she knew things that no proper young lady was supposed to know.

"Why *is* your mother taking you to Brazil?" he asked. Cecily giggled, as though delighted that Jago was curious at last.

"Because Maud is going to marry a rich man! My mother has a second cousin who lives in Rio de Janeiro. She hasn't seen him since they were children, but she's heard that he has recently come into money. Maud is so pretty she'll be able to charm him and then we won't have to steal cutlery ever again!"

"Does this man know you're coming?"

"Mama says he doesn't need to know until she can show him Maud. She's got an ugly little portrait of him in a locket she wears. Goodness, if Maud does marry him she'll be Mrs. Carvalho and then I'll just die from laughing!"

Carvalho . . . Jago recalled the name from somewhere. Wasn't Senhor Carvalho the man to whom old Mr. Piggott had entrusted all his money? Was that how this cousin of Mrs. Conway's had recently become so rich? Jago wondered whether to warn Cecily but he held back, not wanting to alarm her until he could be sure that they were both talking about the same man.

As soon as Cecily skipped back upstairs to ask about the number of Robert Piggott's cabin, Jago pulled out all the letters he had taken from Catherine Piggott's writing case and read each one through in turn. Who was Carvalho, and what was his connection to Armbruster and Catherine Piggott? Jago still intended to speak to Mr. Robert, but first he had to be sure he understood exactly what crimes had taken place.

It didn't take him long to find what he was looking for. A letter to Armbruster, dated 28 July, 1874.

Mr. Armbruster,

It is my wish to be entirely direct with you. I am fully aware of the circumstances of my late father's unfortunate investments and the part you have played in this deceit. You will bring me the key from Casa do Paraiso and you will do

*exactly as you have been previously instructed or I will ensure
that both you and Senhor Carvalho are arrested on charges
of gross deception and fraud.*

Do not underestimate me.

CP

It looked as though Catherine Piggott had found out
about the sewer scam, obviously masterminded by Armbruster and his Brazilian accomplice, Senhor Carvalho,
and had decided to recover the stolen money for herself.
The trouble was, the money belonged to her brother. So
instead of turning Armbruster over to the police she
blackmailed him into a plot to murder Mr. Robert.

Jago folded the letter and rubbed his tired eyes. The
plot hadn't worked, of course. Robert was still alive. But
now it seemed something else was at stake, something to
do with the key that Anna had taken. Did Robert have
any idea what Anna had risked when she gave it to him?
Probably not. People rarely understood each other's
motives, and Jago, right at that precise moment, couldn't
even be sure of his own.

That evening Cecily reappeared with a gleeful look on
her face.

"Cabin nineteen! He's port, we're starboard. I was playing ringtoss with Maud under the awning. I was winning
and Mr. Piggott came up and started to applaud so I asked
him. There was a rather beautiful lady with him. I haven't
seen her before. Then they both came in for dinner and
they were thick as thieves." She smiled, knowingly. "I
expect they're lovers. She kept holding on to his arm."

Jago thought of Anna and felt an old anger rising in his chest. She had trusted Robert Piggott, but here he was with a fine lady at his side. It was just as Jago had feared. Anna had been nothing more than a toy until a richer, more beautiful woman came along. Men like that didn't marry servants—Anna was back in England under Catherine's malevolent thumb while Robert flirted with strangers. How could Jago expect him to help Anna now? Yet he knew that he still had to try to see him. He had made a promise, and Robert surely had a right to know about Armbruster and his sister's murderous plot.

"Cecily, I'm going to try to speak to Mr. Piggott tonight, after dark, when things are quieter."

"Hooray! You've been cooped up down here for far too long. He'll help you, will he?"

"I don't know about that. I'm going to have to ask you to help me again, though. If I'm caught, it'll mean trouble for us both."

"I know! I know! I shall be your scout! I shall go first to make sure that the coast is clear!"

Jago frowned. Cecily was twitching with excitement. She'd never make a conjuror. She didn't have the patience or the stillness of spirit to create an illusion. Nevertheless, he knew he'd be spotted if he tried to prowl about the ship on his own. If Cecily stayed well ahead, then she needn't be involved if he was caught.

"Let's sort out some signals. Hum if it's all clear, but scratch your head if someone's coming. How's that?"

Cecily laughed. "Sounds like something from one of those novels of yours!"

They set off later that evening, at about ten o'clock,

120

after Cecily had told Maud that she was saying good night to Twisty's kittens. She knocked lightly on the locker door, hummed a few notes of a waltz and skipped off down the passageway with Jago following cautiously behind.

Cecily had explained the ship's layout to Jago. He had hidden himself on the bottom deck—the working part of the ship. The forward area beyond his hiding place contained the boatswain's room and the seamen's stores. Behind him lay the coalholes, the boilers and the engine room, with spirits, mail and bullion secured toward the rear. The next level up was called the lower deck, which consisted mainly of passengers' cabins—second class in front of the boilers and first class behind, or "aft" as she liked to call it. Above this lay the main deck with officers' accommodations, the galley and the first-class saloon in the stern. The top deck, or spar deck, was open to the air and used for everything from loading coal and housing animals to afternoon naps in wicker chairs beneath the awning.

Robert's cabin was toward the rear of the ship and about as far away from Jago's locker as it was possible to be. A walk through the second-class saloon was out of the question so Cecily had suggested the open deck, which offered more possibilities for concealment. This meant climbing up three flights of steps and Jago's body ached after his weeklong confinement. Nevertheless, it was bliss to be moving away from his miserable hiding place and he found himself sharing some of Cecily's excitement.

On the landing of the main deck, a door opened and a warrant officer in a blue jacket appeared. Cecily scratched her head vigorously, but Jago had already squeezed into a laundry cupboard across the way. He sat in the dark on a sack full of dirty linen and waited until he heard Cecily humming again. When he opened the door, the companionway was empty. It was almost too easy.

A soft night breeze greeted Jago as he stepped out onto the open deck, and he paused for a moment to inhale deeply. Below deck, the ironclad ship had become a sweltering cauldron in the humid tropical waters. He had spent the past eight days squeezed into a stale, stinking locker, and now he wanted to gulp the fresh air and taste the sea spray. He gazed up at the sky, drinking in its vastness. There was no moon. The only light came from the multifarious scattering of stars and the oil lamps mounted on the corners of the wheelhouse; they cast a pale sheen across the foremast's empty, skeletal rigging, the dark smokestack and the railings that edged the deck.

The fleeting sense of a ship unmanned and adrift didn't last for more than a few seconds.

"Jago!" Cecily was plucking at his sleeve and pointing to where a row of sleeping bodies lay on mattresses beneath an awning. A handful of second-class passengers were camping out. One of the sleepers coughed, startling a goose, which hissed a warning in its crate near the steps. Jago could hear the murmur of voices in the wheelhouse. Now the open deck seemed dangerous, teeming with life and the possibility of exposure.

The two of them crept cautiously along the deck, keeping to the shadows and trying not to breathe as they passed the fowl coops and several pens of restless sheep. They weren't safe in first-class territory behind the funnel, either. The door to the saloon companionway opened and two youngish men in fashionable flat hats stumbled out into the balmy air. Jago ducked swiftly behind a ventilation chimney.

"Not a bad dinner, all told. Mrs. Conway is a fine figure of a woman! Mind you, Morgan put the wind up with all that talk about a storm."

"Can the man be serious?" snorted his companion as he strolled over to the railing and peered down toward an invisible sea. "A hurricane brewing? There's just a bit of a swell. I'd like to hear what Captain Warburton has to say on the matter!"

"If there is to be a storm I'd still put my money on a screw-propeller steamer. We're in safe hands." The second man had joined the first and was struggling to relight a cigar in the rising breeze. "It'll probably blow across to the Gulf, anyway. Oh—hello, Cecily! Off to bed, are you? Regards to your mama, now."

The two men flung their cigars overboard and walked forward toward the bow, disappearing into the dark.

"That was close!" whispered Cecily. "Come on!"

However, as Jago emerged from his hiding place the ship plunged down the side of a deep swell and Cecily lost her balance, skidding on the damp wooden deck. Jago ran to help her, but he too was taken by surprise as a wave crashed against the railing and drenched him with spray. He wiped his face on his sleeve. Was a storm brewing out there in the darkness? Cecily's enthusiasm was catching, but they weren't playing games. For a moment, in the midst of so much turmoil and haste, Jago tasted his own smallness as a mere speck of spume in the vast ocean that churned and heaved all around him. Would it matter whether or not he spoke to Robert Piggott? Would it make any kind of difference to Anna? It seemed unlikely. He gave Cecily his hand and pulled her to her feet.

"What are you waiting for?" she shouted, her words whipped away by the wind. "We're nearly there!"

Nearly where? They were in the middle of the Atlantic Ocean and Jago had absolutely no idea where he was headed.

Jago stood in front of cabin nineteen and hesitated for a moment. The little brass number plate was freshly polished and the lock looked sound, but he wasn't interested in forcing an entry. He raised his hand and knocked.

Jago had sent Cecily away as soon as she had shown him to Robert Piggott's cabin. She had begged to stay, but he knew that there would be even more trouble if she was seen with him so he stood there alone, waiting for the door to open. He had no idea what he was going to say. He'd have to make it up as he went along.

"Wait a minute. . . ." He heard the muffled voice of a man from somewhere on the other side. "Is that my hot water?"

Jago looked down, suddenly nervous. Someone was coming along the narrow passage to his left. He could hear the rustle of skirts and the murmur of nighttime voices. Why didn't Mr. Robert open the door? The voices were drawing nearer. No one was going to mistake him for a second-class passenger—in his filthy rags he was clearly a stowaway. The key was turning in the lock at last, but already it was too late. He had been seen.

"You there! What do you think you are doing?"

Jago turned. Mr. Morgan was hurrying along the passageway toward him. Mrs. Conway was beside him, clutching his arm.

"Goodness, Mr. Morgan, I do believe it's that boy from the docks!"

"Catch him!" shouted Mr. Morgan as a perplexed looking Robert Piggott peered into the passage, but Jago didn't hang around. He knew the drill. Run and hide. His response was as mechanical as the throb of the machinery in the engine room below, as the shrill ringing of alarm bells in his head and the fearsome, thunderous pounding of his heart.

Jago had the advantage of youth and the benefit of experience. He knew there was no point in heading down to his old hiding place. The cupboards and stores were bound to be searched first, boxes and trunks hauled out of holds and every dark corner investigated for signs of a stowaway. The passenger decks seemed little better, for everyone would be on their guard against a filthy boy whose crime was unmistakable on a ship with no emigrants, no working folk, no steerage class. He began to run back up toward the open deck with a view to crawling into one of the little lifeboats that dangled out from the bulwarks, but he knew already that these too would be searched once the alarm was raised.

"Jago!" A voice hissed at him from behind the door at the bottom of the companionway. He swore under his breath. It was Cecily of course. He should have known she wouldn't do as she was told. Her familiar shape slid out and grabbed his hand.

"Come on!" She was like the stick that always came back. He had no option but to follow her as she flitted across to the starboard passage.

"There's no point . . . ," he muttered, not wanting to draw her any further into the chaos that surrounded him, but Cecily put her finger to her lips, noiselessly unlocked a door and pulled him into the darkness of an unlit cabin.

"Maud is asleep," she whispered. "Get under her bunk. She snores horribly, but I promise that no one will find you. Mama will come along soon. Don't make a sound— you'll be all right."

And so Jago found himself crawling under a bed, squeezing once more into a dark, cramped space with no room to move, no fresh air to breathe and no hope in hell of escape this time.

14
Overboard

Jago was woken by a hand reaching for a chamber pot three inches from his right ear.

"Oh Mama . . . I feel absolutely dreadful."

"Well I didn't sleep a wink with all that commotion outside, and I'm sure the boat is tipping up and down far more than Captain Warburton led us to believe it might!" It was Cecily's mother speaking. Jago recognized her theatrical tone. He wondered whether to crawl out and show himself. It was he, not they, who had spent the night on tenterhooks, listening to the shouts of the crew and the stamping of feet as they searched the ship for a young stowaway. Cecily had been quick to speak to Mr. Morgan from behind the Conways' locked cabin door, assuring him that Maud had been in bed all evening, that no one could possibly have entered without her knowledge and that such questions did little to help her poor mother's nerves. As Mr. Morgan apologized and promised that the search would continue elsewhere, Maud and her mother settled back into their bunks and were soon snoring peacefully, as Cecily had predicted.

Yet for Jago, the noise of a ship being turned upside down had persisted all night. There were other sounds too—the sound of a girl sobbing in the cabin next door and the sound of a man banging his fist against something, growling angrily at her to shut up. Later he heard other voices through the thin partition wall—the urgent murmur of an argument and the angry cadence of muttered oaths. Someone was clearly upset about having his cabin searched.

Jago felt like joining in the cursing. How could he have been stupid enough to think that he could take a walk through the ship and remain unseen? Why had he thought that Mr. Robert would believe anything he said? He should have stayed in the locker, or better still, stayed on the dockside in Southampton. Jago's old life in England seemed eerily distant, yet not two weeks before he had been with Callow at the fair on the hill. He felt a sudden stab of loss—not for Callow, but it felt like grief all the same. Walking through a grassy field, the sun on his neck and a passing crowd to please . . . That was where he belonged. That was home.

Jago's chest felt tight. He'd forgotten how to cry. He had learned early on that Callow saw tears as a sign of weakness to be exploited to the full so he'd kept his emotions hidden, always believing in something better, something beyond his meager life that kept him safe inside himself. Yet now he didn't try to shake off the fog that enveloped him. What was the point? It seemed there was no way out as his lonely tears leaked into the ditch he'd dug around his heart.

By eight o'clock the next morning he felt completely empty. He lay there quietly, drifting on the steady tide of Mrs. Conway's complaints. She seemed to take the bad weather personally. However, any thoughts of giving himself up were pushed to one side as a more immediate problem presented itself. Maud was searching for her dressing gown.

"Look under your bunk, you silly girl!" scolded Mrs. Conway. "That's where you usually throw it!"

"I'll look!" Cecily was speaking. Jago saw her hand grope toward him under the sheet that Maud had tossed aside. His muscles tensed. She'd be in trouble if he was found. He wasn't going to let her take the blame. He grabbed the wrap he had been using as a pillow and stuffed it into her searching fingers.

"Here it is!" she announced to her mother and sister.

"Hmm. Thank you," sniffed Maud. "Oh no—it's all damp and grubby! I can't wear this!"

"Well don't wear it then!" Cecily sounded exasperated. "Why don't you get dressed properly and we'll all go and have some breakfast?"

"I thought I might just take some tea in bed." The wooden frame above Jago's head creaked as someone sat down.

"Come on, Maud—you'll feel so much better once you're up and about. . . ."

"Yes, do get up, Maud." Mrs. Conway was speaking now. "I was hoping you'd distract our lovely Mr. Morgan so that I can pop a pair of those rather fine butter knives under my shawl."

"Oh for heaven's sake, Mama . . . must you?" Yet Maud was standing up and, after a further tortuous half-hour of dressing and brushing and fussing, Mrs. Conway and her daughters were gone.

Jago crawled out and stood up, leaning into the angle

of the tilting floor. He was in a smallish cabin with two bunk beds curtained off to one side. There was a washstand, a corner cupboard, a sofa, two chairs and a table, plus a great deal of clothing and bedding and clutter. It looked as though Cecily had been sleeping on the sofa. She would be back soon no doubt, loaded down with tidbits from the breakfast table and gossip from the other passengers about the stowaway her mother had seen. Jago peered out of the small round window. The sky was gray and the inky sea was dashed all about with white-capped waves. A shower of spray spattered suddenly across the glass. He stepped back as a trickle of water leaked down the wooden paneling.

Jago leaned across Maud's bunk and put his ear to the wall. Nothing but silence accompanied the now-familiar creaks as the ship plowed through the waves. The commotion from the night before had died down, it seemed, and most passengers were surely breakfasting in the dining saloon by now.

The boat dipped suddenly and veered to port. As he put his hand out to steady himself Jago's fingers brushed against something that lay between the folds of the eiderdown. It was a locket—solid silver by the weight of it and inlaid with black jet. A trinket like this would have been prime pickings for Callow. Jago expertly flicked the catch and the locket sprang open to reveal a cloudy daguerreotype of a dark-haired young man. Cecily had said that her mother wore a locket containing the portrait of Senhor Carvalho. Was this the villain who had conspired to steal the Piggott fortune? The pose was stiffly formal and entirely unremarkable except for a shadow that darkened the man's skin beneath his left eye. It might have been a birthmark, or a large mole. He closed the locket and put it back on the bed. It wasn't the sort of face to please a girl like Maud.

Jago stepped across the little cabin and tried the door. It had been locked from the outside. In the corner stood Mrs. Conway's padlocked trunk and he sat down on it, uneasy about making himself too comfortable. He needed to think.

On a half-empty vessel like the *Colorado* it was only a matter of time before he was found. Maybe that didn't really matter, but in the morning's gray light he was ready to reconsider. Cecily had risked a great deal to hide him, and Anna's bruised face had returned to haunt his dreams. He would have to try to reach Mr. Robert one more time. Afterward the captain could do what he liked with him. There was just one problem. How was he going to move about the ship now that everyone was searching for a stowaway?

The room began to tilt quite sharply. Jago looked up. The trunk he was sitting on was gradually sliding across the floor as the ship lurched sideways, riding out a giant swell. His legs and his stomach had by now adjusted to the constant roll of an ocean-bound steamer, but as a book on Maud's nightstand slid to the floor he recalled the words of the man up on deck the night before. Was a storm brewing? Cecily had said they were only a couple of days from the equator. A storm in the tropics might be dangerous. The crew would have to lash everything down. They would have to be on their guard against damage or loss of any kind. Things could get washed overboard in a storm. . . .

Someone was turning a key in the door. Jago jumped up, but immediately he heard Cecily's whisper.

"It's only me!"

She came in and handed Jago some buttered rolls and a cup of milk.

"I said I wanted to look for Twisty's kittens. She's moved them somewhere—the dining saloon was too noisy, I suppose. Anyway, Maud wanted to come back too, but luckily Mama persuaded her to stay. Mama's the center of attention. Having a stowaway on board has definitely livened up the conversation, and they'll probably sit there till luncheon."

Jago took the food.

"You know I can't stay in here, don't you? They'll search the ship till I'm found."

"But you can't let them find you! You haven't sorted out your trouble with Mr. Piggott or those letters yet, or anything!" Cecily looked so anxious that Jago forced a smile.

"What if they don't think I'm on the ship anymore? What if they think I've fallen overboard? They'd stop looking for me then, don't you think?" He sat down again on Mrs. Conway's trunk and bit into a roll. "I'm not going to hide under your sister's bed for the rest of the voyage. I've had an idea. . . ."

Jago explained that if any of the passengers or crew thought that they had seen a body hit the water, and if Cecily swore that she had seen a young lad climbing on the railings, then the search for the stowaway would be over. First, however, they needed to make a body double and somehow get it up to the spar deck without being seen.

It was easy enough to fashion a head and a torso from a large white pillowcase tied off with one of Cecily's hair ribbons. The legs were more difficult, but a pair of woolen stockings were eventually found among Mrs. Conway's things and they did just the job. Cecily stuffed the limbs with rolled up newspaper and soon looked quite pleased with her handiwork, but Jago shook his head.

"If we throw it overboard like this, it'll be carried off by the wind, or blow back in our faces. We've got to weigh it down so that it falls straight into the water and sinks, just like a real body."

"Weigh it down with what?" asked Cecily.

"I'm not sure. Books?"

"Mama would soon miss her *Langdon's*. She'd smell a rat. It's got to be something that won't be noticed for a while."

Jago's eyes began to wander around the room looking for suitable objects, but Cecily was already leaning forward.

"How about some cutlery?" She patted her mother's trunk. "Even if Mama does miss it, she'll never be able to report it."

"Are you sure?" asked Jago, but the idea of throwing all her mother's ill-gotten gains into the sea rather appealed to Cecily.

"I never did think much of all that thieving," she explained. "Mama's not very good at it. She's bound to get herself caught sooner or later. The cutlery is nothing but a burden."

Nevertheless, despite Jago's own feelings on the matter he found himself resisting her logic. He hadn't told her what he knew about Mrs. Conway's Brazilian cousin.

"If your mother loses the silver then you'll be even more dependent on the hope that this Senhor Carvalho will marry your sister! I'm not sure . . . Cecily, what if Carvalho is a thief himself?"

Cecily looked up from her work and smiled disarmingly.

"Then we'll have to set him back on the straight and narrow too, won't we?"

So it was settled.

Jago made Cecily look the other way while he used a needle from Maud's sewing box to pick the padlock on the trunk. He didn't want to be responsible for teaching her any more bad habits. Nevertheless, he gasped when he opened the lid. The trunk was full of solid silver knives, forks and spoons, many of them monogrammed or engraved with intricate family crests. Each piece was carefully wrapped in its own little square of silk and laid between layers of petticoats and bed linen.

"Blimey!" he murmured. "This should be enough to drown me!"

Cecily had learned that the captain wished to address all the adult passengers in the main saloon before lunch, in order to quell the rumors about a hurricane. At midday, therefore, the coast was relatively clear. Jago threw Maud's hooded traveling cape across his shoulders and bent down to pick up his odd-looking bundle. It was heavy all right, but would anyone believe it was him?

"Cecily, if anything goes wrong, will you do something for me?"

"What do you mean?" Cecily, Jago knew, wasn't the type to imagine failure of any kind. He shoved his hand deep into his trouser pocket and pulled out Clara's long-hidden letter-block.

"I want you to take this."

"What is it? Oh, I see—*J* for *Jago!*" Cecily took the little piece of type and looked inquiringly at him. Jago sighed.

"It means a lot to me. Please, just look after it."

He knew he owed Cecily a proper explanation, but there wasn't time for questions he didn't think he could answer. He pulled the velvet hood over his head and opened the cabin door. It was time to go.

The two of them stepped cautiously into the passage and Jago walked as lightly as he could toward the stern companionway. It wasn't easy clutching a jangling dummy under his cloak. Up on the next landing, one of the doors to the main saloon was slightly ajar. As they approached, the hum of voices drifted toward them. The room was full of passengers waiting for Captain Warburton to speak. Jago's plan was to drop the stuffed body over the railing so that it would be glimpsed by someone near a porthole in the saloon below—a fleeting apparition of arms and legs before it sank beneath the waves.

They crept up the stairs; Jago could hear the wind whistling under the door at the top. Someone, however, had seen them.

"Miss Conway! Miss Cecily! Don't go up on deck now! It really is too rough to promenade!"

Cecily turned around.

"Hello, Mr. Morgan! I'm . . . Maud just needs to take a couple of deep breaths to clear her head—we'll be back down directly!"

"I really don't advise . . ." But Cecily was already climbing the stairs and Jago, wrapped in Maud's long cloak, did not look back.

Up on deck the wind was whipping spray and rain in all directions. Cecily went first. She walked toward the smoking funnel and turned and waved to show that the coast was clear. Jago took a deep breath. They had talked about the best position on the deck, where each of them would stand and how they would signal to each other. However, as he emerged from the companionway the cloak he was wearing billowed out around him, restricting his vision and unsettling his orientation. The deck was tipping away from him as the ship toiled through the waves. Was the wheelhouse in front of or behind him? He knew he had to stay out of sight of the duty watch, and he began to drag the stuffed dummy in what he hoped was the right direction. When he reached the side he hauled the bundle up so that it dangled across the railing. The legs flopped heavily. It already had the look of a broken body.

Jago turned and looked back toward Cecily. She was shouting and waving, but her words were carried away on the wind. One final push and the bundle would tumble into the sea. Then Cecily would run downstairs to confirm that someone had jumped overboard. However, Maud's cloak was blowing everywhere, getting in the way. He pushed it back from his head and at that moment caught sight of someone hurrying across the deck toward him from the edge of his vision. It wasn't Cecily—it was a man wearing the blue coat of a ship's officer.

Jago hadn't expected this. He turned and crouched down behind a skylight. The rain was driving into his face. He was panting, catching at his breath before the wind could whip it away. It was impossible to think straight on the storm-washed deck, yet he needed to act fast. He needed to vanish.

The officer would have seen a figure wearing a woman's cloak. The art of illusion, Jago knew, lay in planting a tiny seed that subtly blurred the boundaries of perception and interpretation. With trembling hands he shrugged off the velvet folds and shook them into the wind. The fabric billowed out, but he held on, shielded like a housemaid pegging out a sheet. Just inches in front of him the stuffed body dangled limply, jackknifed by the railing. Jago raised his foot and kicked at the sodden bundle, flipping it over the edge so that it tumbled down toward the sea. At the same moment he let go of the cloak. It ripped away from him, yanked up into the air by the gusting wind. In another second it had caught in the ropes of the mainmast rigging, where it twisted and flapped like a tortured bird.

He heard shouting. With what seemed like an agonizing slowness Jago scrambled into one of the little wooden lifeboats that dangled out over the bulwarks, sliding beneath the oilskin cover and pulling it back over his head. Cecily was screaming that someone had fallen overboard. The officer would be looking over the side, watching for a body, searching for any sign of life in the white-capped waves below. Perhaps he would catch a glimpse of a pale cotton sleeve before it sank without a trace, but this would be over in a matter of seconds. Then the officer would raise the alarm.

"Woman overboard!"

15
The Steward

"Miss Cecily! Cecily!" Jago could hear Mr. Morgan's voice, shouting through the wind. "What happened? Was that your sister who fell?"

"My sister?" Cecily repeated the question, sounding a little puzzled and yet somehow strangely calm. Her voice had a high, clear quality that carried through the roaring interference all around. "Oh! No, no—Maud isn't here . . . there was someone else. . . ."

"Who? Who was it?" insisted Mr. Morgan, but now Jago strained to catch Cecily's reply for she began to cough, choking out her words.

"That boy. The stowaway!" Suddenly she was sobbing, her voice shaking, overcome with distress at what she believed she had seen. "It's too terrible to bear! Jago—I think Jago has drowned!"

Almost immediately Jago heard other voices, shouting, giving orders. Someone was comforting Cecily. As she was led below, Jago realized that his connection with her had been severed. She had spoken his name and betrayed the fact that she knew who he was. And yet, without knowing it, she was making him safe. The illusion he had created had succeeded too well. When Maud's cloak was taken by the wind, she believed that she really had seen him fall. There would be an investigation; the captain would question her and she would say whatever she felt she must, but she did not know that he had not drowned.

Jago lay in the lifeboat for over two hours. There was no question of a rescue being attempted—the ship would not be able to turn quickly enough and the strongest swimmer would have been lost in moments among the giant walls of water that rose and fell all around.

The lifeboat itself swung out over the ocean with every lurch and roll, but Jago stayed there, exhausted and wet and strangely exhilarated. No one knew he was alive. He had become himself again, master of his own actions, dependent on no one and nothing but his wits. Cecily had fed him, brought him information, and made him laugh, and he hoped desperately that she would be strong enough to be true to herself in the interrogation that would surely follow. Yet for Jago's next few hours he needed to act alone.

Jago opened the door to the laundry cupboard and slid quickly inside. He'd left a trail of wet footprints in the passageway behind him, but there was nothing he could do about that. The quicker he changed out of his sodden clothes and into his disguise, the better. Only a tiny amount of light entered the cupboard from under the door, but he knew exactly what he was looking for—a sack full of dirty linen that he'd noticed as he hid there the day before. He fumbled with the drawstring and rummaged around until he had found a smallish white jacket that buttoned to the neck and a pair of crumpled maroon trousers. The clothes were too big of course, but Jago rolled over the waistband of the trousers and stuffed Catherine's letters into the pockets of the jacket to pad it out a little. He smiled grimly. Baggy jackets, he knew, had many uses.

Next he tackled his filthy face and hands. His own wet clothes made a facecloth of sorts and he chewed at his ragged fingernails until he could pick at the dirt that lay underneath. He even gave his old boots a rub though no one was likely to notice them under the drooping hem of his trousers. After slicking his wet hair down with his fingers he felt as ready as he could be. He pushed open the door and stepped out as a rather small, slightly soiled steward of the Royal Mail Steam Packet Company.

Jago walked back along the starboard passageway toward the first-class accommodations. More than anything he wanted to run, but he knew that running would give him away. Instead he tried to move like a steward; shoulders back, hips loose to counteract the motion of the waves. The ship was wheezing and creaking all around him as doors banged and bells sounded: two men in engineers' overalls emerged from the right and pushed past him, hurrying below to check their pressure gauges and redouble the efforts of man against the sea. The floor beneath him lurched forward suddenly and Jago put out his hand to steady himself against the wall.

"You there!" A man's voice rang out sharply behind him. "Lost your sea legs? Stop weaving about like a pansy and take this tray down to cabin twelve!"

Jago hesitated, but only for a second. He had no choice but to turn and take the tray. Fortunately the man dressed in kitchen whites strode back into the galley without giving him a second glance. Now, however, Jago had to walk like a steward *and* carry a tray loaded with cups, a teapot and two plates of sandwiches.

Another steward ran down the steps ahead of him and maneuvered past with a large crate full of empty bottles. Jago continued on, flushed with relief and adrenaline. He was beginning to feel more confident. Perhaps everyone else was too preoccupied with the storm to take any notice of a ham-handed novice in a dirty jacket? He had already drowned, and something that Callow had inadvertently taught him was that the key to a great illusion lay in deceiving his audience's expectations. If he was dead, he couldn't be serving tea in a first-class cabin, could he? Jago would deliver the tray, but not to cabin twelve. He had a different destination in mind.

The passageways around the first-class cabins were dimly lit, and it took him some time to find cabin nineteen. Jago knew that he was taking a huge risk, but he had to find out more about Mr. Robert's intentions. He knocked, then stepped back with lowered head to what he hoped would seem a respectful distance. The door opened immediately. Jago held out the tray.

"Oh! Was tea ordered? Bring it in then." Robert Piggott stood back from the door and waved him in.

Jago stepped into the cabin and tried to walk calmly toward a little table, but his hands were trembling so much that the teaspoons clattered in their saucers. Fortunately, Robert had turned away and was sifting through some papers in his portmanteau. Jago had rehearsed his speech while he cleaned himself up in the laundry cupboard, but now that he was finally here the words seemed to stick in his throat. He put down the tray and gave a little cough.

"Oh yes—here." Robert turned around and held out a shilling. Jago hadn't planned on a tip. He took a deep breath.

"Sir, I don't want money. I must speak to you about . . ." He paused. Robert wasn't listening. He was looking over Jago's shoulder toward the doorway. With a shiver of dismay Jago realized that he had forgotten to shut the door behind him.

"So, you have found your sea legs at last!" said Robert. "Well, don't stand in the passageway."

A man's thick-soled boots clumped over the threshold.

"She wants the key, Piggott."

It was Armbruster. His voice was unmistakable, spitting consonants and rudeness like a spring-loaded automaton. Armbruster had been on board the *Colorado* all the time, suffering from seasickness by the sound of it, and confined to his cabin. Robert, however, seemed to have been expecting him. Whose side was he on? Jago ducked his head and circled around the table, suspicious now of everything except his need to flee. Yet before he could reach the door he heard the soft rustle of an expensive dress.

"Tea first, Mr. Armbruster. Then business." Catherine Piggott spoke quietly, her cool restraint a chilling contrast to Armbruster's impatient bark. Jago felt the hairs rising along the back of his neck. He shrank into the shadows behind the door and watched her sweep into the cabin in a gown of shimmering silk moiré—black for mourning, yet hardly the somber crepe of a grieving daughter. Robert hadn't found a lover—he'd found his sister.

"Darjeeling, I trust," said Catherine, lifting the lid of the teapot. Jago began to edge around the door, but she turned and touched him lightly on the shoulder. "We haven't finished with you yet. Stay and pour, please."

Hiding his face beneath his flopping fringe, Jago obediently moved toward the table though his heart was hammering so loud he felt sure that someone would hear it. He didn't know how to pour tea. He lifted the little milk jug and knocked it clumsily against the sugar bowl. Robert Piggott was speaking.

"Catherine, my dear, what about a little privacy? I am determined to get to the bottom of this business, and of course, I am delighted that you felt able to join me at the last minute—Casa do Paraiso is your birthplace as well as mine—but really I fail to see why Armbruster needs to be involved. If he had done his job and advised Father against the Rio scheme, then we wouldn't need to be on this cursed boat at all!"

Armbruster coughed. Or was it a growl?

"Robert, Mr. Armbruster just wants to make amends. He speaks Portuguese—he will help us find the old house and deal with the caretaker. Wait!" Catherine had walked over to the table and was watching Jago. "Never put the milk in first!" She picked up a cup and saucer and handed them to her brother. "One simply cannot find good servants these days."

"You do very well with Anna, Catherine," said Robert, drinking some tea.

"Ah yes, the irreplaceable Anna! You may as well know that I intend to let her go. She took something from my bureau, you know. . . ."

"You know perfectly well that she took the key from Casa do Paraiso and gave it to me. She stole nothing. She gave me what Father had intended for me. Don't you remember what he used to say? 'When I am dead, you shall reap my life's fortune.'"

Jago knew that he ought to put the teapot down and leave, but now he busied himself with straightening the teaspoons, desperate to hear more.

"Well, the poor, untrustworthy little dear is still feeling ill and will not improve, I don't suppose, until we reach Rio." Catherine stared intently at Robert. "Anna will remain in my cabin—there is no need for her to retire to the servants' berths. You cannot see her. Understand, Robert, that I know all about your ridiculous little flirtation and I will not countenance it! I'll ruin her first! However, if you give me the key, then perhaps we might forget all about it. . . ."

Jago peered out from under his fringe. Catherine and Armbruster had both moved toward Robert, circling him, closing in. Armbruster was nearest and Jago found himself looking at the disfiguring scar beneath his eye. It wasn't like a cut, or a burn. It almost looked as though a piece of his flesh had been gouged out. Frostbite, maybe, or a tumor. It might even have been made by the removal of a characteristic feature, like a birthmark or a mole. . . .

Robert was speaking again.

"You find it so convenient to forget things, don't you? I simply cannot believe how you had that young stowaway hounded until he drowned! And then you laughed and said he'd got what he deserved! I don't understand you, Catherine." He put down his teacup. "It's a little too stuffy in here for me. I'm going upstairs for some air." The door was still open. Robert stepped neatly around his sister's skirts and, either through ignorance or instinct, escaped into the safety of the passageway.

Catherine shut the door behind him, blocking Jago's exit. Jago instantly lowered his head, but there was no one to deflect attention now. He dreaded her turning toward him, querying his age, his size, his demeanor until she recognized him at last. It was time for a diversion.

A wave flung itself against the grimy little window. As Catherine glanced over her shoulder Jago stuck his foot out and tugged sharply at the rug on which the table and the tea things stood. The table wobbled and the tray crashed noisily to the floor.

Catherine raised a finely plucked eyebrow as she surveyed the broken crockery.

"How careless!"

"I'll fetch a broom," mumbled Jago.

"Yes, you do that," she said, opening the door for him. "You might also try to find yourself a better-fitting jacket."

Jago looked up, startled, and found himself staring into her steely gray eyes. He tried to look away but found that he could not, his gaze transfixed by an intensity he felt powerless to resist. It seemed as though her black pupils were boring into him, mining his secrets, sifting through the half-forgotten fragments of his dreams. He had faked his own death, yet this alone did not make him invisible. Could she see beyond his disguise?

Catherine laughed abruptly, breaking the spell. Jago shook himself out of his daze. She wanted him to go.

"Au revoir!" she murmured as she closed the door behind him.

Jago stumbled along the empty passageway, neglecting his steward's gait while his mind absorbed the details of what he had just seen and heard. Catherine had not spoken his name. She had looked him in the eye and let him walk away, and in his relief he pushed aside the impression that she was playing a cruel and clever game. If she had any suspicions at all, then surely she would never have let him go. No—it seemed as though he'd gotten away with it, and in the meantime he'd learned that Anna was on board, that Robert had not betrayed her and that both Piggotts put a high value on something at Casa do Paraiso. Also—Armbruster had a scar where the young Carvalho's mole had been. The pieces of the jigsaw were beginning to form a picture. Only one or two details were still missing. What was locked away at Casa do Paraiso and why had everyone risked so much for it?

Jago headed for the dining room. He needed an audience. He wanted to challenge Catherine and Armbruster in a public place in front of witnesses who would judge him on the evidence alone. It wasn't the dinner hour yet, but if he could examine the room beforehand, then so much the better.

In order to reach the dining room, he had to cross the

main saloon. He lurked in the doorway for a moment, plucking up the courage. Half a dozen children were hurtling about among the potted plants, bursting with energy after too long at sea and hunting for mischief while their mothers and nannies embroidered and worried about the growing storm. One or two gentlemen snoozed determinedly behind old newspapers and a steward was busy anchoring card tables.

The clock on the wall showed four o'clock, but the shutters had been closed to keep out the storm and the flickering oil lamps cast a dirty light about the room.

Jago picked up a pile of folded napkins from a little service stand and tried not to stagger as he crossed the tilting hall toward the double doors of the dining room. Dinner was at five, he knew, so he needed to find somewhere to hide until all the diners were seated.

The dining room appeared to be empty. He walked in, shut the door behind him and looked around. This room was even darker than the saloon. Its long, narrow shape gave the unsettling impression of a coffin in the gloom. The low ceiling was split by a shuttered skylight through which filtered a few chinks of light from the open deck above, while a large ceiling fan creaked around and around, powered by steam pipes from the boiler amidships. Sturdy wooden benches ran down either side of a long central table. Canteens of cutlery sat on the top of a large mahogany sideboard against the rear wall, and racks of bottles and glasses hung suspended from the ceiling by thin brass rods. Jago guessed that the stewards would come in to set the table at the last minute, to avoid any breakages as the ship lurched about.

A little alcove near the sideboard was curtained off with a drape of heavy brocade. Jago crossed the room and slipped behind its folds. He was just in time, for as he did so, he heard footsteps and the sound of a door handle turning. Someone must have entered. He caught his breath as the curtain twitched suddenly and something brushed up against his trousers, but it was only Twisty, purring as she recognized the intruder.

"Sssh," he whispered, picking her up and stroking her. The cat felt soft and velvety warm, yet soon she was wriggling free. Her kittens must have been close-by. She slid beneath the brocade folds and disappeared. Jago leaned back against some crates of wine and waited in the darkness. The minutes ticked by.

By a quarter to five the stewards had arrived to light candles and straighten tablecloths. The settings were placed swiftly, and before too long, benches were scraping as diners took their seats.

Jago peered through a tiny slit between the curtains. Catherine, Robert and Armbruster had already arrived. They were seated next to Captain Warburton, a few feet away from the alcove. The chief steward hovered behind them, his back close to Jago, his keys dangling importantly from a chain. If Jago slid his arm out he might just be able to reach them. . . .

Mrs. Conway entered with Maud and a red-eyed Cecily. A man Jago recognized as Mr. Morgan stood up and beckoned them over to a bench near the door. Other diners were seated about, some a little greenish as they contemplated the cold slab of liver pâté on their plates, but there were many empty places.

Captain Warburton stood up and said a short grace.

"My congratulations to you all for tolerating the inconvenience of such inclement weather. Let us drink to the good health of those among us with more delicate constitutions and, please, enjoy this excellent dinner with me!" He raised his glass, but his toast was interrupted as Cecily abruptly stood up.

"What about Jago?" She looked pale and wide-eyed in the flickering candlelight. "He may have been an inconvenience to you, but now he is dead and I don't know how any of you can even think about eating!"

The other diners stared at her. One or two had the grace to look embarrassed.

"Sit down!" hissed Mrs. Conway, tugging at her daughter's arm. "Don't be absurd!"

"You have had a difficult day, my dear," soothed Captain Warburton. "Calm yourself—there was nothing any of us could have done to save that poor, sad soul."

"Well I think there is something rotten going on. Jago knew about it and then he drowned, but he won't rest until it's settled. I saw his ghost cross this room just an hour ago!"

Jago closed his eyes for a moment. Cecily must have stepped into the room when he hid behind the curtains. She had probably been looking for Twisty's kittens. Now her faith in him had to be repaid.

It was time to begin.

16
The Key

"Good evening, ladies and gentlemen!" Jago pulled aside the heavy curtains with a bold sweep and bowed to his audience. "Compliments of the *Colorado!*"

Faces turned toward him. Mrs. Conway uttered a little shriek of surprise, but before anyone else could react, Jago moved swiftly toward the table and picked up an empty wineglass.

"Don't be dull! Drink and be merry!" He swept his other hand down the front of the glass and, with a flourish, revealed it to be full of dark red wine.

"I say!" exclaimed the young man to whom Jago offered it. "That was rather well-done!"

Captain Warburton was clapping.

"Excellent! Who arranged this? It's just what we all need!"

Jago looked toward Catherine. She was sitting absolutely still, watching him, her gunmetal eyes unblinking and unfathomable. Cecily's reaction was easier to read.

"It's Jago!" she exclaimed. "It's his ghost! I told you I saw him, Mama!"

Jago moved quickly around the end of the table and stopped behind Cecily.

"Look what I've found!" he whispered, leaning forward to reveal three tiny mewling kittens in his cradled arms.

Twisty had moved them to an empty crate behind the curtain. They had enjoyed their little sleep up his sleeves.

"Oh . . ." Cecily took the kittens, too stunned to speak.

"It's all right—feel my hand. Too warm to be drowned!" Jago spoke quickly as he dropped something into her lap. "Listen—this key is the chief steward's master key. Take it and unlock the door to the cabin next to yours. Have you still got my letter-block?" Cecily nodded, her bright eyes fixed on his. "Good. Give it to the person inside and tell her to come as quickly as possible. Go *now*."

By this time the rest of the diners were beginning to wake up to the fact that the stowaway was still alive, after all. Benches scraped back as people stood to get a better view. Mr. Morgan was on his feet, edging cautiously toward him. At the same moment a heavy hand gripped Jago's shoulder so tightly that he winced as thick nails dug into his skin. Armbruster's hot breath was on his neck.

"Not a word. Not a bloody word . . ."

Captain Warburton, meanwhile, was weaving around the diners toward Jago and Armbruster.

"What on earth is going on?"

Jago turned his head to check that Cecily had slipped away through the open door.

"Don't let me spoil your dinner! Begin, please!" He reached around for a napkin and handed it to Maud. She stared blankly at him. Armbruster tightened his grip.

"Shut up!"

But Maud was remembering her manners. She shook the napkin out across her lap. A stained and crumpled piece of paper floated to the floor. She bent down, curious to see what it was.

"A receipt . . . ? Oh! Look, Mama! It is signed by Senhor Carvalho!"

Armbruster seemed taken aback. With his free hand he grabbed another napkin. A second piece of paper fell out of its folds. Maud picked it up.

"Carvalho again! Why are his receipts hidden in the napkins?"

Captain Warburton was examining a third napkin, and a third receipt. He looked at Jago.

"What the devil are you playing at?"

Jago took a deep breath.

"I'm not playing, sir. I think I can prove that the criminal behind a substantial fraud is at large on your ship."

"Shut your mouth!" snarled Armbruster, like a foxhound held back from a kill. "You can't prove anything!"

"Let the boy speak!" insisted the captain.

Jago twisted around and wriggled free from Armbruster's grasp.

"Sir, these receipts show that a Senhor Carvalho received tens of thousands of pounds from an old man with a soft heart who felt guilty about a fortune built on the profits of the South American slave trade. When Carvalho wrote to ask him to invest in a scheme to build underground sewers for the people of Rio, the old man jumped at the chance. Yet those poor Brazilians never got their clean streets or their perfumed gutters, for the scheme was a hoax set up to cheat the rich out of their money."

"No! Oh no . . ." Mrs. Conway was groaning, eyes closed. Maud began to fan her with her napkin. Another receipt fell out. Jago continued.

"The money seemed lost to a criminal gang on the far side of the Atlantic Ocean—too far for the long arm of the law to claw it back. The old man died shortly afterward, broken and ashamed."

"A sorry tale indeed, but I should like to reassure all the passengers that there is no one by the name of Carvalho on board the *Colorado*," said the captain loudly, looking around him. He beckoned to the chief steward. "Take the boy to one of the empty cabins and lock him in. I'll deal with him later."

The steward took Jago by the arm, but Jago wasn't ready to leave.

"Got your keys?" he asked. The steward looked down and gasped in horror at the chain dangling loosely at his side. Jago took the opportunity to turn toward a dazed-looking Mrs. Conway.

"Mrs. Conway, I think you may be able to clear this up. You have a locket belonging to your cousin Senhor Carvalho, don't you?"

"I . . . how do you know about that?" she stuttered, completely bewildered now.

"Please—may I?"

Mrs. Conway fumbled with the necklace around her neck. She unfastened the clasp and handed it across the table.

Jago opened the locket. Inside lay the murky image of a young man with a mole beneath his eye. Yet it wasn't the picture that convinced Mrs. Conway as she trembled before Armbruster's thunderous scowl.

"It's him, isn't it?" she whispered, ashen faced. "He used to frown at me like that when we were children. . . ."

Jago placed the locket down on the tablecloth. She did not pick it up again.

"I wanted Maud to marry him. I haven't seen him since I was eight. I had no idea he was on the ship!"

Armbruster, however, had clearly heard enough. Plates of pâté went flying as he leaned over and smashed his fist down on the telltale portrait.

"Well, well, well! So you are Margherita Conway! I can see the family resemblance!" He pulled his lips back over his gums in an ugly sneer. "I've heard all about you, cousin! You and your charming ways with other people's silver. . . . Captain Warburton—this woman is a thief! You cannot believe anything she says!"

"How dare you!" Mr. Morgan stepped forward now, cheeks flushed. "I insist that you apologize immediately!"

Before the two men could come to blows, however, someone else was standing up. Robert Piggott looked tired and drawn, but his voice was steady as he spoke.

"Captain Warburton, I believe this young boy is telling the truth. I have no idea how these receipts came to be in his possession, but if Mr. Armbruster is Senhor Carvalho, then he is, I regret to say, a thief. Our father was completely taken in by him. Wouldn't you agree, Catherine?"

Catherine, Jago noticed, had been listening very quietly to everything that had been said. Her hands were folded in her lap. She looked perfectly composed—even faintly amused.

"I fear it must be true, Robert. After all, the evidence is compelling. We must applaud the actions of this young boy in bringing Mr. Armbruster's deception to our attention."

"You bitch!" roared Armbruster, furiously kicking over a bench as he struggled against Mr. Morgan's restraining armlock.

"Take him away!" ordered Captain Warburton. "I will not allow such language in front of the ladies!" Two stewards ran forward to help Mr. Morgan and, with much swearing and shouting, they managed to push the apoplectic Armbruster out through the doors.

Jago's heart was pounding in his chest. He gripped the edge of the table in front of him as a wave crashed across the open deck above, drowning out all sound until from somewhere down below a bell began to ring. Captain Warburton turned to face the remaining diners.

"Forgive me, but I am needed elsewhere!" he shouted. "Mr. Piggott, may I prevail upon you to watch the boy until I can speak to him later? I suggest that everyone else retire to their cabins. We may be in for a long night." He turned and strode out of the dining room, followed by a handful of pale-faced passengers.

Seawater was trickling down from the battered skylight above. Several candles had been extinguished in the draft, deepening the gloom.

"Oh dear me! Where is Cecily? Maud, some water . . ." Mrs. Conway was fading, yet she and Maud were Jago's only witnesses now. He needed them to stay. Stepping forward, he deftly removed something from Robert's breast pocket. It was a small, delicately shaped brass key.

"What . . . ?" Robert looked shocked, but Catherine merely smiled, as though she'd known it was in his pocket all along.

Jago palmed the key and opened out his hand to show that it had gone. Then he leaned across, extracted the key from behind Maud's blushing ear and tossed it up into the air. It landed at Catherine's feet.

"Very pretty!" she murmured as she bent down to retrieve it. Yet before she could touch it, Jago pulled his arm back and the key flew up into his hand, attached by a hook to an invisible string.

Catherine sat back, her face in the shadows. She said nothing, but her hands were clasped tightly together, the bones of her knuckles stretching her pale skin. Jago dropped the key into a glass and with one swift movement vaulted his slight frame up onto the table.

"I think it's time for another little story," he began. "You see, old Mr. Piggott had two children. When their father lost their inheritance to an overseas scam, Robert showed his temper by throwing away the old man's watch. Perhaps some of us might have done the same. But Catherine here was different. She sniffed out the villain behind this foul-smelling fraud, yet instead of telling her father, now on his deathbed from the shock of his losses, her mind twisted itself toward evil ends and she began to blackmail Armbruster. She knew that if she went to the police, her brother would inherit the recovered money. She, however, wanted it all for herself."

"This is outrageous!" spluttered Robert, but Catherine gave a tight little laugh.

"The boy is a thief, my dear. Let Captain Warburton deal with him."

"And which is the greater crime?" asked Jago. "Theft, or murder? She tried to have you killed, sir. When that didn't work, she arranged for the death of an old man she reckoned was in the way."

The wind moaned like a merman down the narrow ventilation shaft. Robert was clutching the last of the candelabras. He held it up to peer at Jago, and in the flickering glow he looked bewildered, and afraid.

"Who *are* you?" he asked.

"I . . ."

Another wave crashed against the starboard windows, and Jago grabbed the wooden rack above his head. For the first time that evening he faltered. Where was Cecily? Without her he could prove nothing. He had run out of tricks.

Catherine's face slid out of the shadows and she stared at him as he swayed in the gloom. He tried to look away, but her eyes drew him in like a full moon on an ebb tide until all he could see were two points like dark tunnels leading him forward, over the edge, falling away into silence. His limbs felt so heavy. There was nothing to cling to and no one to save him now. Better to submit, better to go under. . . .

"You are a thief." Catherine was speaking. "Tell my brother that you are a thief."

She made it seem so easy. Nevertheless, she had miscalculated.

With his last ounce of effort Jago scrunched his eyes shut. The wind was competing for his thoughts, howling under the leaky skylight and yammering in his ear like a sullen old man: *Don't look 'em in the eye, boy, or they'll skin you to the bone.* Maybe Callow had taught him a trick or two, for now he was remembering, reminded of something he'd seen a thousand times in murky tents at country fairs—con men playing mind games with soft-brained marks to win bets and drink away the takings. Of course. Hypnotism was her hidden card, and like a fool he'd failed to read the signs.

He snapped his eyes open.

"I am Jago Stonecipher!" he shouted, pointing toward the doorway. "I am a conjuror!" Catherine's face shriveled into a sneer, but it didn't matter anymore. He too had an ace up his sleeve.

Quick as lightning Jago leaned forward, blew out Robert's candle, grabbed a carving fork and in one swift movement thrust it sharply upward. There was a loud hiss like a bitter sigh as he punctured the steam pipe that ran along the ceiling above his head.

"Oh, a light, please!" begged Mrs. Conway, but by the time Robert had relit his candle and held it aloft, the room was transformed. A gray mist hung in the air like a luminous miasma, obscuring faces and softening shadows. The fan had stopped turning.

A young woman's cry confirmed the illusion.

"Jago!"

Faces turned toward the door. Robert gasped as Anna appeared, emerging from the vapor like a wraith. She looked skeletal in the dissipating steam; her eyes were sunken and her bony hands fluttered up to a purple bruise on one side of her face. Cecily was supporting her arm.

"You must sit down," insisted the younger girl, guiding Anna toward a seat next to her mother. "She was lying on the floor, Jago! She couldn't get up at first! I don't think she's seasick, I think—"

"Anna! What has happened to your face?" Robert was pushing benches aside, trying to move forward. "Who did this to you?"

Anna turned away from Robert's outstretched hand and looked up at Jago. As he stared down into her haunted eyes the anger he had kept at bay now rose up from his chest and threatened to choke him. She had been locked away in Catherine's cabin for ten long days while her mistress and Armbruster tried to squeeze the truth out of her. She hadn't given in, but now, in front of strangers, she needed to know that it was all right to speak. Jago swallowed and nodded gently to her. She looked back toward Robert.

"It was your sister," she said. "Because I gave you the key. Robert, your father told me things about the key, about Casa do Paraiso. I was with him in his last hours. The delirium he suffered helped him to unburden himself, I think. His mind was so troubled. I'm sure he never meant for things to end like this."

"I think you should explain yourself in full," said Mr. Morgan, returned to check on the passengers. "There are many reputations at stake."

"Yes, well, and none more so than that of old Mr. Piggott," Anna continued. "He felt so dreadful about the part his father had played in the South American slave trade, yet he loved Brazil—he had married his wife there. They bought a house called Casa do Paraiso, where Robert and Catherine were born. But his wife died of yellow fever, and Mr. Piggott, sick of the slave blood on his hands, shut up the house and left for England."

"The key, you see, belongs to a safe hidden deep in the

cellars of Casa do Paraiso." Robert was keen to take up the story. "Our father always told us that a family treasure lay buried there. He told me that when he died, I should take the key and recover the fortune myself."

"Yes, and what about me?" Catherine was breathing rapidly, her lungs visibly struggling within the confines of her corset. Tiny beads of sweat glistened at her temples. She gripped the bench in front of her. "Why should I not share in the family wealth? Father always favored you, and when little miss lovelorn here took the key from my bureau, it was only right that I should seek to get it back!"

Anna was trying to speak again, but the room tipped forward abruptly and her voice was lost beneath the cries of Mrs. Conway and the cacophonous crash of cutlery and crockery. A bell began to ring from the passage beyond the hall. Catherine lunged forward, all composure gone.

"I only want what's mine!" she shrieked as Jago stepped in between her and Anna. "The girl is a servant and she should be punished!"

"No, wait, there is something else you don't know!" cried Anna, cowering behind Jago, clearly terrified of her hard, cruel mistress. "There is no fortune at Casa do Paraiso! Not money, anyway. . . ."

"Liar! My father would never have confided in a servant!" spat Catherine as she reached forward and tried to slap her.

Robert took hold of his sister's arm and pulled her down into a chair.

"Leave her alone! What do you mean, Anna?"

"Forgive me for not telling you," pleaded Anna. "I think your poor father mistook me for your mother. I didn't know what to do . . . there was so little time."

"What did he say?" demanded Catherine, her perfect complexion now mottled with rage. Anna couldn't look at her. She spoke only to Robert.

"The key opens a box that contains a lock of hair and the wedding ring that belonged to your mother. She was his 'life's fortune.' The only people who mattered more to him were his children. I think he feared that if he told you there was no money you would never return to Casa do Paraiso."

"No!" screeched Catherine, but instantly her cry was drowned by a bone-splitting crack that seemed to rip open the very core of the ship. Jago was flung from the table and hit his head on a bench as the dining room veered to forty-five degrees. Glass and porcelain were smashing all around as the sea gushed in through several gaping shutters.

"My God—the propeller shaft's gone!" muttered Mr. Morgan, the blood draining from his face as he ran from the room. The floor was awash with napkins and bottles as water swept across the boards and splashed around the table legs. Cecily crawled under a bench after a terrified kitten.

"Are you all right?" she asked, staring at the gash on Jago's eyebrow. Jago, however, had glimpsed a long black train being dragged through the flood. Catherine was heading across the saloon toward the aft companionway.

"Don't go up there!" he shouted, but whether it was the howling wind or Catherine choosing not to hear him, she didn't stop. Her skirts caught for a moment against the door frame and she tugged them impatiently, ripping the silk until she was free.

"He won't have it. No one will have it!"

Jago splashed toward her.

" . . . throw it in the sea. Let it sink to the bottom . . ." She was muttering. Her damp hair had loosened from its elegant arrangement and was plastered like seaweed across her face. She had reached the top of the companionway and sharply wrenched open the door. Water cascaded down the steps and almost knocked her off her feet.

"Come back!" yelled Jago, struggling up the steps behind her, but she was already on the open deck.

He met the storm head on as he crawled out after her. The sky was bearing down now, battering the ship in a frenzy of water and wind. Catherine was clinging to the skylight and staring wildly around her as a huge wave crashed across the deck. Jago lost his balance and was swept backward against the aft hatch. By the time he had wiped the stinging salt water from his eyes, Catherine had crawled over to the railings. Now, however, the deck began to roll sideways as a giant swell rose from the port side. An empty fowl coop tumbled toward the stern and smashed against the capstan. Catherine tried to get to her feet, but her waterlogged skirts kept getting in the way. She was sliding toward the gangway opening. There were no railings on that part of the deck—just a rope slung across the two-foot gap.

Jago grabbed a plank from the broken fowl coop and leaned forward toward Catherine.

"Take hold!" he shouted, but she didn't seem to notice him hanging on to the railing behind her.

"Take hold!" he yelled, determined not to have to witness another death. But Catherine wasn't like Callow. She didn't want to be saved. With an agonizing slowness she slipped farther toward the gap. Her fingers were clawing at the deck, but when she turned her head and looked at Jago, her eyes were full of loathing.

"Don't touch me!" she screamed. "You came from nowhere and you are nothing!"

Jago dropped the plank and lunged forward. He grabbed at her arm, but with a sudden shock he felt her fingers grasp his ankle, pulling him down. She was trying to take him with her. They were sliding overboard together.

Jago twisted around, his fingers scrabbling for something to hold on to. His feet were already dangling in the black vacuum between the ship and the sea. Catherine was shrieking incoherently, writhing and kicking at him with her pointed little boots. She wanted him to die. As her right arm let go of the deck and she slid toward the water her fingernails dug into his leg. But Jago didn't fall with her. Strong hands were grabbing him beneath his shoulders, pulling him back, and a gruff voice was shouting furiously above his head.

"You can't drown twice! Not on my ship!"

It was over.

17

The Artist

Jago stood in the bows of the *Colorado* and looked out across Guanabara Bay. It was the most beautiful place he had ever seen. The broad arc of coast was dotted with islands like iridescent jewels. From the jagged green skyline to the west towered the giant tooth of Mount Corcovado, while the softer bulk of Sugar Loaf Mountain rose straight from the water's edge. The red-tiled roofs of Rio clustered prettily along the shore, and all the while boats of every description—tugs and schooners, paddlewheel steamers and fishing barks—danced in a choreographed flotilla through a sparkling sapphire sea.

"Look at all those little boats!" Cecily laughed as she pointed out the landmarks to Jago. "They seem to be following us!"

The *Colorado* had been badly damaged in the storm. The propeller shaft had splintered under the strain, causing complete engine failure and almost sinking the vessel. It had been touch and go at the pumps, but somehow the masts had remained intact, and as the storm weakened, the sails were raised. Captain Warburton relayed the news of Catherine's death by cable from Pernambuco, and the ship limped south for a further ten days before reaching Rio. Now, however, the *Colorado* was causing quite a stir as rumors of her misfortune spread across the harbor.

The sun was warm on Jago's neck. He was wearing his

old clothes, but Mr. Morgan had lent him a cap, and he pushed it back now to take in the view.

"I think I shall like living here," said Cecily. "Mama says there are waterfalls!"

Mr. Morgan had asked Mrs. Conway to marry him. It seemed he'd known about her light-fingered habits from the start, but he'd fallen in love with her anyway. Mrs. Conway vowed to mend her ways, and Maud was delighted at the prospect of piano lessons and a house in shady Santa Teresa.

A light breeze brushed Jago's face and he breathed deeply, still relishing the joys of the open deck and the freedom to stroll wherever he pleased. His thoughts turned to Anna, who was resting below. She would bear the scars of her ordeal for a while yet, it seemed. Jago had no idea whether she would ever marry Mr. Robert, who for the moment was entirely taken up with his return to England to salvage what he could of the Piggott family fortune. In the meantime Anna was to live with the Conways in their new home. Mr. Morgan had offered her the position of companion to Maud and Cecily, "to keep those girls out of mischief," as he put it.

Cecily was tugging on Jago's arm.

"Can I be your assistant?" she asked, her eyes widening at the sheer superlativeness of the thought. "You'll need one when you're famous!"

Jago smiled. It was clear that Cecily had no intention of becoming a young lady just yet.

"Your mama says you must apply yourself to your lessons."

"Yes, but if I get bored I shall jump out of the window!"

She grinned mischievously. "I will find you, Jago Stoneci-pher!"

As Cecily skipped below for breakfast, Jago tried to imagine his own future. Captain Warburton had offered him his passage back to England if he agreed to enter-tain the passengers. Yet what if he chose to stay in Brazil? He had always longed for the chance to begin again, to build a life away from Callow's skulduggery. Nevertheless, England still had a hold on him. His past lay there—everything he had ever been. Most of all it was Clara's resting place.

Jago tried to picture his sister. He hadn't thought about her much over the past few days and it didn't seem right. He no longer heard her voice and now her face was fading too. He took out his letter-block and toyed with it in his hands, palming it just as he had always done.

"Stand by there! Get your cable out and your anchor clear!" Captain Warburton was striding along the spar deck, barking out orders. The *Colorado* had finally reached port. Down on the cobbled quayside, dark-skinned men grappled with giant ropes the size of the boa constrictors Mr. Morgan had warned him about. Brown-eyed women in elaborate turbans heaved huge baskets across their shoulders and gabbed in a language Jago didn't understand. Beyond the sprawl of ware-houses, strange trees sprouted broad fans of greenery. Bright flowers tumbled over every inch of sun-bleached wall, and everywhere, all around, the overwhelming smell of the city rose up to greet him: coffee and sugar-cane, fish and feijoada, sweat and the unmistakable stink of the sewers that flowed into the sea.

"Senhor! Senhor!"

A trio of wild-haired children were jumping up and down on the harbor wall below. They giggled and pointed, and though Jago had no idea what they were saying, he waved back and bowed. He didn't need words. He didn't need talismans either. His sister's spirit was free now, no longer bound by the ties of his own grief. With a flick of the thumb he tossed Clara's letter-block up into the air and, in the half second before it fell, he had pulled a peach, a pebble and two bread rolls from his pockets. The children cheered as he began to juggle. His hands moved faster and the items flew higher, round and round until everything blurred in a bright ring of breathtaking speed.

Jago smiled. His wasn't the magic of deceit or rivers of blood or shivering and fear; his audience was his family, to be taken by the hand and drawn into a transfigured heartland of wonder and delight. He clapped his hands and the rolls and the fruit tumbled toward the children. The pebble landed in his open palm and he watched the letter-block as it fell in a gentle arc toward him. He didn't catch it though. The metal flashed like a smile in the sunlight and then it was gone, swallowed up by the narrow strip of water that separated Jago from a new continent.

"This is the age of science! Come closer! Draw nearer!" he shouted, opening out his arms as if to embrace the whole world. "The conjuror uses simple mechanics to amuse and entertain you! Yet wouldn't you rather travel farther, suspend your disbelief, open yourselves to mystery? I am an artist. I will take you beyond what you see and what you know. I will teach you how to unlock the power of your own imaginations. I will show you how to fly. . . ."